KINGS ON THE ROOF

BY SHANE HARRISON

Short Stories

Blues Before Dawn
The Benefits of Tobacco

Novel

The Testimony of Virginia McCabe

KINGS ON THE ROOF

SHANE HARRISON

First published in 2020

by Forty Foot Press

www.fortyfootpress.com

Cover Design and Layout by A.J. Gatsby

Set in 11pt Baskerville

A CIP record for this book

is available from the British Library

ISBN: 978-1-916248205

CONTENTS

To my parents

Veronica and John

THE FIGURINE

Daniel considered himself a man of taste. Over the years he had cultivated a temperament in harmony with his inner self, one that satisfied his cultured appreciation of art, order and dignified inexuberance. Fireworks might rain through the air, drunks and lovers might shout and carouse in the streets, but Daniel could smile to himself, confident that his outer shell held his inner calm inviolate.

That is not to imply that he was aloof from life or that he was fastidious in that unsettling way that marks the dictatorial and the insane. He could be outwardly jolly. For instance, when shopping for fruit and vegetables in the marketplace, he was not above trading banter with the stallholders. He would stroll with his pretty wife, Hortense, arms linked in the companionable afterglow of love, sharing private jokes and hailing passing friends.

Their apartment, spacious and expensively furnished, was much frequented for dinner parties and soirees. Amongst the set of creative and intellectual people with whom they mixed, it had the status of a salon. They themselves had no children, a mutual agreement allowing them to pursue their lives unburdened by care; free to indulge their taste for fine art, fine wine and exotic holidays.

Yet, for Daniel, the true bliss of life was solitude. An evening stroll through the emptying city was an almost daily pleasure, the bare metropolis itself adding piquancy to his reflections. An aperitif sipped at an unobtrusive table beneath the plane trees in the square was a frequently taken option. He delighted in the park with its manicured imitations of nature, whilst keeping himself an island oblivious to the consoling idiocy of its honking animals and children.

However, his principal retreat was within his own home, within his own designated den with its air of sombre certainty. It was a small room, windowless, containing only those sparse accoutrements he desired. Crowded bookcases lined two walls; an ancient bureau occupied the third. A leather armchair stood as a throne in the centre, a small reading table and a standard lamp adjacent. There were a few objets d'art by way of decoration, or more by way of indication that here dwelt a man of taste. His degree in the liberal arts was framed and hung alongside an abstract lithograph by an eminent local artist. There was also a large photograph of a group of friends at an elegant city bistro, glittering women and smooth, smiling men raising their glasses in some unspecified toast. Beside the door, a slim cabined set into the wall contained more objects: a debating award, a plaque with sports medals, antiques, jewelry and other assorted bric-a-brac that were, for the most part, souvenirs from numerous foreign holidays.

The overall effect was tasteful yet somehow reassuringly homely he felt. Although... although... Perhaps he was still that little bit short of the effect he was aiming for. Exactly what that was he could not quite clarify in his thoughts, but something rather less contrived and more suggestive of spontaneity, or a certain rakish verve was needed.

On a day when these thoughts were to the fore he was interrupted, not for the first time, by an animated, cheerful intrusion of Hortense's. He brusquely dismissed her but immediately felt bad about it. This brief guilt, visited upon his prior bliss, was unfair. She must know that he delighted in the gloom, found it the epitome of the soul, saltier than the sweet but brief taint of happiness. Hortense must insist on attempts to make him smile, only causing him to glower all the deeper at her intrusion.

As she withdrew he swallowed the oath in his heart and attempted a reconciliation, but on this occasion she was not to be mollified. So it was that Daniel left the apartment that evening a little off-key with the world, a nonspecific feeling of distraction or asymmetry lying heavy on his spirits.

He took a table on the terrace of a popular bar, the Sunset, just off the Plaza of the Angels. He ordered a Mojito which he felt would be conducive to gaiety and, when it did not prove so, ordered another. The word 'millenarianism' occurred to him and the insight raised a slight smile to his lips. Fool of a woman, he thought.

There was a movement at his shoulder and he started on seeing a tall, gaunt black man approach his table, tawdry wares and trinkets held out on his spindly arms. There was something else though. Beyond that sensation of mere surprise, he sensed a drumbeat behind the wide eyes of the hawker, a reflection of a cloud drawn across the moon, furtive shapes pulled from the darkness of the earth.

Daniel shooed him away but, ever so briefly, his eyes were held by one of the gewgaws proffered by the black man. It was a figurine no larger than a hand, indistinct in its rendering and in terms of its utility. Nor indeed could its gender be defined, the net effect of body and face being somehow androgynous. Seduced and repulsed in turn, Daniel was conscious of his pupils dilating, conscious of a quickening of his pulse. The black man noticed too.

He gave his name as Mamadou. Such a detail as a name was seldom noted for someone of his status; a street shadow, a stain in the crowd. Yet his teeth shone and his eyes lit up. He became transmuted in sparks, like the gentle motion of lights across a dancehall ceiling.

"Sir, you like this, maybe ..."

Daniel shooed him away again. He could not allow the negro to assume access to his mind. How dare he! It was not a question of racism, Daniel told himself. He considered it oafish to liken the dark race to monkeys, to argue that if Europe had no population of one it could do without the other. What of Gibraltar, then? Yet one had to consider that Gibraltar was distinctly odd. One had to acknowledge that it was correct to accept separation of the twain, to remain singular and aloof.

Daniel frowned. His thoughts were unworthy, garbled, the two drinks having more effect than anticipated. The auguries of the evening not being any more auspicious, he set sail for home. He took the shorter, busier route, along a wide thoroughfare known as the Avenue of the Saints. Whatever the original motivation, this had become something of a misnomer, being lined with hawkers' stalls, fast food trailers and the like, many manned by Africans and others from the margins: beggars, buskers and idle youths, lounging with aggression and hailing passing strangers. Five minutes on and the Avenue crossed another thoroughfare just as piously and inaccurately named – the Avenue of the Blessed Virgin. On an island in the busy intersection a statue of the Virgin, cast in weathered bronze, stood atop a globe, a snake trapped beneath her feet. Despite the years of neglect, still she bathed the street with her benevolent gaze.

The lights at the junction were broken, causing a jam of pedestrians. Two municipal policeman with batons were giving a frantic floorshow, conducting the flows of traffic and pedestrians with sweaty artistry. Drawing close to the kerb, Daniel noticed that the black man from the Sunset Bar, Mamadou, stood immediately ahead of him. This proximity felt uncomfortable in an odd way, as if smirking fate was determined to maintain contact between them. Daniel was close enough to see the jewels of sweat on the man's temples, smell the southern spice of his body odour. Yet, despite himself, he drew a magnetism from these things too. Daniel was compelled to step closer.

There was a sense of impatience growing amongst the pedestrians, a quickening heartbeat as they collectively anticipated their cue from the policemen. The crowd pushed forward. One of the policemen turned. Daniel noticed a brief hiatus, that split second where everything froze as time strove to press inexorably on, everything, that is, except for the black man who took a step forward onto the street. That one footfall set everything back in motion. However, the pedestrians remained poised, realising that the policeman's action was not directed at them but at another flow of traffic. Mamadou realised this too late; he stood transfixed on the road in the path of a screeching bus. Daniel saw it all in intense detail: the old municipal bus, battered and grimed, faces lurid with horror floating behind its windows like so many dead fish, smoke billowing from tyres as the brakes locked, such details as were inherent in the situation. What disturbed though was the serenity of the black man before the monster's approach, inexplicably greeting his inevitable demise with a calm smile. A smile, Daniel noted, that looked for all the world like gratitude.

Daniel reached out and grasped the black man by the scruff, pulling him back to the safety of the pavement as the bus skidded by. Another scream died away while the anger and horror that had been building amongst the crowd dissipated in curses and laughter. The policemen, realising their error, allowed the pedestrians across, some of them allowing looks of contempt to rest on Daniel and Mamadou who remained on the pavement.

The black man was intense, if not quite effusive, in his thanks. "How can I repay you, sir? I was a dead man for sure."

Daniel noted that the man had dropped something which now rested at their feet. He hunkered down, an instant before Mamadou did likewise, and seized the thing first. The two men rose together, Daniel with the figurine resting easily in his palm.

This trinket ..." Daniel tossed the figurine in his palm and shrugged, rather as if he did not care so much.

Mamadou grabbed his wrist, "No," he said, firm as his grip.

Daniel forgot his distaste for such unwarranted contact and smiled. Perhaps it was ungenerous to take the black man's thanks so literally. After all, he was a poor man and Daniel was rich, relatively speaking. "Relax, my man," he said, "I simply meant that I will buy it off you. How much is it you sell these things for, five dollars?"

Mamadou released his grip, hesitation crossed his features, then faded. "Thirteen dollars," he said.

Daniel raised an eyebrow. Too much for a trinket, then, but not so much as one might pay for an objet d'art. Should he haggle, offer ten, perhaps?

"Thirteen," Mamadou repeated, persuasive if not quite threatening. "It is worth a lot more."

Daniel doubted that. He had seen similar gewgaws at the various African stalls and markets dotted about the city, on mats spread on every second sidewalk. They peeped out from amongst the cheap jewelry, the pendants, potions and spells with their vague promise of southern magic, secret powers. But this one, this one; it fitted so snugly in his palm it was as if it always belonged there. Anyway, the suggestion that the black man was indebted to him seemed suddenly absurd.

"Thirteen it is, so." Daniel took some notes and coin from his pocket and handed the correct amount to Mamadou. "Thank you," he said.

"No, thank you." Mamadou smiled.

Briefly, Daniel thought he detected a strange edge to the smile. He realised too that the man was slightly older than he had first thought, thirtyish perhaps, where before he had assumed a mid twenties drifter. There was a stature about him as well, exhibiting more poise than one would have expected from a denizen of the streets. In parting, the man made a gesture with his hands, a gesture that suggested to Daniel the giving of benediction. Then, brusquely, he turned and strode away along the Avenue of the Blessed Virgin.

Daniel waited for him to merge into the dappled light before looking at his figurine. His figurine! He felt elated, sensing the blood in his veins coursing with a vigour he had not experienced for years. With a furtive glance about, for which he couldn't quite account, he put the figurine away in an inside pocket. Something was changed, a fundamental warp in the ether. The black man, if his change of direction could be so interpreted, had clearly decided against going home and so would he. The night was young. He would trace the Avenue in the other direction, infiltrate that notorious district beyond, returning home when it suited him.

Daniel established the figurine in a prime place in his cabinet. Set at eye level and slightly off centre, it did not dominate yet succeeded in completing the display. One's eyes were drawn to it, not immediately but eventually, as though it were the natural focus, waiting for due attention. Daniel decided that this illustrated the joy of recognition; that the space had always awaited the figurine which itself had bided its time before taking up its destined occupation.

This coincided with a reinvigoration within Daniel himself. His soul expanded and demanded it be filled with more and more stimuli. He sought new experiences, expanded his enjoyment of the arts beyond the rarified and rather staid constraints of yore, experimented with new foods, with drink and other, less legal, stimulants. He sought the pleasures of a more eclectic society, immersing himself in the company of strangers, outsiders and subversives, all the time adding to his own wealth of character.

Or so it seemed to him. Within his own established company there was little reciprocation of these new appetites. Friends were dismayed by his excesses, trying to still his enthusiasms with silence, ultimately with absence. Hortense also withdrew, becoming over time a shadow forever fading in the glow of his radiance. He barely noticed at first, then he hardly cared. She had not aged well, Hortense, a fact which was an aesthetic subtraction from the dash Daniel liked to cut. He noticed all the more how he stole the eyes of younger women, women who had once found him invisible, indeed who now opened more than their eyes to him. Such suitable company he could find in the bars and casinos where he generously cast his money each night.

Daniel spent less time in his den though it remained a refuge for him. He would spend some nights slumped in the chair sleeping off the excesses of a particularly Bacchanalian session. Always he noted the figurine and felt a mutuality in the connection. There it stood, sentinel to the now unchanging display of the cabinet, observer of little more than falling dust, an immobile smirk suggested on its tiny features.

Time passed. Hortense grew grey before withdrawing permanently to the house of a sister living in the Sierras. Daniel, hair a youthful black, his skin radiant, did not mark her leaving. Everything in his life was now detached as though viewed on a monitor. The memories of his wife, his friends, his work quietly buzzed below his consciousness, no more discernible than the muffled sounds sometimes heard from adjacent rooms. The upkeep of his apartment became a chore, its consequent neglect a growing cause for irritation.

These negative undercurrents reflected themselves in the mirror of Daniel's existence. He found himself looking into unfriendly faces, hard eyed faces that no longer appreciated his qualities. Peevish, carping criticisms pursued his rare essays into work so that he was forced to free himself of the burden of employment. There were surely more immediate concerns for a man such as he, those pressing matter of joy to be found at the racetrack or casino, in bars and bordellos throughout the city. He was, after all, surrounded by youth, suffused with it. Clouds scudded across the sky, traffic flowed through the streets like flood tides, posters shouted slogans and faded, paint peeled.

Daniel sat at his favourite bar and recognised not a soul. The staff had grown solemn and aloof, the patrons, more often than not, were insular, shunned. He wondered where all those young families had gone.

A face, faintly familiar, loomed above him. The waiter – what was his name? – proffered a drink, a golden aperitif which he set down, deliberately on the table. Daniel raised an eyebrow.

"With the compliments of the house," the waiter said.

"Most kind," said Daniel – such loyalty he commanded. Still, why did the man linger?

"We are used to it, Señor. For some time your drinks have been on the house," the waiter paused for effect, "but your account has not been settled."

Daniel raised both eyebrows. He waived a hand dismissively, "It is being dealt with."

"But of course." Still the waiter paused. "It is just that this drink must be our final compliment." He bowed and withdrew.

Daniel raised his drink to his lips. It was true, he had been negligent with his affairs. All those bills, those demands, that pestered him like a conscience each day, how persistent and unsolvable they were. An unspecific imperative suddenly gripped him, ominous in its very vagueness. The city hurried by without acknowledgement but somewhere out there he fancied that he saw a black face clarify from the throng, saw it turn and regard him for an instant, in contempt, in dread.

The streets parted and flowed. Humanity, sunshine, the scattering leaves pulsed through the thoroughfares past the static figure of Daniel who remained as a rock in the unceasing torrent. The imperceptible motion of his walk bore him onwards, taking him at last to his familiar apartment.

How derelict the neighbourhood looked, desolate even, as though its occupants had fled leaving what remained to the dispossessed and the wrecker's ball. Surely this district was fashionable once, its windows brightly blinking, showing off their reflections of style and success. The elegance of its architecture, adorned with ornate sculpture, which had once delighted the eye now seemed faintly ridiculous. A grey coating muffled the sheen of glass, stone and steel. The drunk and ribald statuary teetered on parapets, making a mockery of their classical support. Those few people on the street moved slowly, in pain or despair, shrinking within their shabby clothes. Graffiti was everywhere, the coils of writing, symbols and obscene cartoons, growing like weeds over the wall; for all its exuberance, speaking more of absence than anything else.

Daniel found his door, fumbling with forgotten keys until he had it open. A fetid store of air embraced him. Sweat prickled on his neck as he stepped across a floor of envelopes, dust and powdered glass. Did he not live here? Could he live like this? His den was stripped of most of the accoutrements of comfort. Gone were the lithographs and jewelry, gone too were those technological toys that had once seemed so necessary, so desirable. Some photographs remained, souvenirs of a more personal than any pecuniary merit. His diplomas also survived – laughable, really – but the bitter half-smile forming on Daniel's lips froze as his eyes came to rest on the figurine.

How long he stood there, his eyes held captive by the wretched thing, he could not say for certain. Nor would his thoughts ever connect to anything articulate concerning it. He would have to take action but could not imagine what, nor indeed how he might ever navigate the vast nothingness that had colonised his intellect. All he could feel was that he was a stone washed by the eternal tide, that he would in time, in far too much time, erode to nothing – a final, ironic physical symbiosis with his soul.

Back out on the street Daniel surrendered himself to the flow, was carried along by it to his destination. It was all he could do. At the Plaza of the Angels he sent a plea for directions into the ether and the angels flexed their wings. Onwards, they seemed to say, their stone bodies marking a pathway along the skyline. At the Avenue of the Saints he followed the line of hawkers' stalls arranged in meaningful perspective, saw saints shine from the faces of beggars and gesture him helpfully on. At the Avenue of the Blessed Virgin he stopped at last with sharp recognition, for he remembered that this was where it had all begun.

Daniel alone looked to the statue guarding the thoroughfare as the crowds passed sightlessly by. The Virgin still stood atop her globe but less demurely than he had remembered. Her leg, clearly defined beneath her bronze garb, was thrust slightly forward to lend her pose an air of suggestion. The serpent she had once crushed was now seized in her hand with all the wanton connotations that implied. Daniel looked to her eyes, seeking out the love that had resided there, the love for all the denizens of this blasted city. Did she not love them anymore? Did she not love him? Her face formed itself curiously into the features of Hortense - oh, half remembered yet everpresent - her eyes looking through him with blank intensity.

"Where should I go?" Daniel pleaded, and then he knew. It was not the virgin that pointed but the sinuous coils of the snake. Stretched sinfully along the sculpted stone it showed the way to the darker quarter of the city. At least, it was once the darker quarter. Daniel expected the mean streets of old but these expectations proved groundless. The walls were whitewashed and clean, bougainvillea flowed from rooftop gardens, date palms sprang up from sheltered courtyards, all drenched in dappled light and exotic scent. Here the older buildings retained their dignity. Paint and metal were elegantly worn while newer additions were quietly elegant, strong but unobtrusive.

At length Daniel came to an area of newly built apartments nestling into the foothills at the edge of the city centre. A brief premonition set its tremors within him so that he looked up to the second floor of the newest block to see a black face looking down at him. He knew that this was Mamadou and knew also that he was not being regarded surreptitiously; he was expected.

Mamadou's apartment was large, airy and spartan. The fading light flooded it, coating all surfaces with a brassy monochrome. His host was reduced to a silhouette, shimmering like a wraith, guiding him through corridors and rooms with minimal gestures. Daniel arrived in what appeared to be the dining area. A sparkling, modernist kitchenette was arrayed along one wall of glass and chrome. Another wall of glass framed the city while the remaining two were bare. The floor was all pale boards, highly varnished, without an item of furniture upon it.

Mamadou had laid out a spread on an ornate rug set squarely in the centre. There was a blinding array of foodstuffs in small individual helpings, their colours a heady rainbow against the dark weave of the rug and the monochrome of the apartment. Pickled eggs in a stone bowl, giant tomatoes stuffed with rice, saucers of figs, plates of couscous suffused with spices of different colours, jars of pickled fruit and bottled oils, wooden bowls of varied salads, green, purple and yellow leaves glistening against the last of the light. There were other foods Daniel did not immediately identify; a tapioca with a stirred red spiral the colour of blood, a shredded orange meat in an ochre puree, strange scallops, a fantastic spectrum of sauces. It was a savage display, yet somehow touching in its fastidiousness. There was something womanly there, a tendering of sensuality inherent in the offering, but Daniel had seen no evidence that the black man possessed a woman. He deduced that this was another aspect to the deceit of the hustler, as if Mamadou had somehow accumulated all the human facets for no other reason than to bury his beggardom.

Time had certainly passed since last they met. Mamadou's hair was dusted grey, his skin now rumpled, marked with arbitrary dark splodges. He was old, perhaps even older than he looked, especially about the eyes. With one brief gesture at the feast, Mamadou folded himself gracefully to sit crosslegged and begin to eat. Daniel fighting impatience, reckoned that to be agreeable might expedite matters. He sat heavily, took an egg and consumed it with ferocity. The spices made his eyes water, so Mamadou's image wobbled like light on water, went from old to young, then olden again.

They ate in silence for a time, using their bare hands, each throwing occasional guarded looks across the rug. Mamadou looked the happier of the two, relaxed within his own space, consuming portions with an air of nonchalance. He was the first to speak.

"You are looking well, my friend."

"We were not friends that I recall." Daniel flicked some grains of couscous from his fingers. "But you, time has not ignored you in its passing. On the other hand, though yes, you have aged, you have … all of this." He gestured to their surroundings which, while spartan, spoke of comfort.

"Such possessions are the benefits of prudence," Mamadou replied. "It's something we learn with time. We need time. What time had I for acquisitions when I had to seize every waking moment to trade? I was a whirlwind. You, my friend – yes so I do regard you, a friend who freed me from the captivity of youth."

Daniel sneered. He reached inside his jacket and took out the figurine. "And this is a token of our friendship, I suppose? Take it! Yes, take it, my friend. My gift!"

Mamadou looked away. "It was destined to belong to you." His eyes returned to Daniel's. "And you to it."

Daniel was incredulous. "You speak to me of destiny? You, a nigger in the dark, a whoremonger tempting the unwary with his wares."

"If you recall," Mamadou replied, "You followed me. By the Angels, and the Saints and the Blessed Madonna."

Daniel stood, enraged. "I saved your life!"

Mamadou smiled with sad satisfaction. "Did you?" He stood too, with some effort. "And did you ask me? No sir, you did not. But this thing you show me, that was our mutual object, was it not. Perhaps you heard it calling you." Here, Mamadou did a strange thing, making his voice tiny: "I am yours, Daniel, come to me."

"Nonsense!" roared Daniel. "You are an African, you sell gewgaws. This, this thing, you foisted on me by way of thanks. Well, no thank you. You can have it back." Daniel's grip on the figurine tightened so that he felt a flange of power flow through him, felt a reluctance to make good on his offer.

"It is not for giving. Remember?" Mamadou held up his hand, then rubbed forefinger and thumb together. "For purchase always. Eh, thirteen dollars?"

Daniel's laugh was sour. "You are not on my gift list. Owe me the money, if you care, but take it back!"

Mamadou shook his head. "I got it at an old antique shop in an alleyway off the Markets. A run down, neglected place, but crammed with the most fascinating flotsam and jetsam of the world, a whole raft of curiosities. From the start I had my eye on the figurine, of course, but was somehow unable to ask for it."

"I daresay you find your life interesting, but I..." Daniel shrugged, made a face to show he did not care, but his eyes betrayed that face.

Mamadou smirked, held up his palms, then continued. "The shop was run by a gypsy woman; intense, inscrutable, unapproachable. I was attracted of course, and haunted the place. Yet we never spoke, only our eyes. I was going to, surely I was going to, when fate intervened.

"One evening, I was walking along the alleyway when I noticed smoke escaping from beneath the door. The hero in me emerged; I charged in, somehow found the stricken gypsy woman and carried her from the shop. I laid her on the street where she remained immobile for a while, her arms crossed, clutching something tight to her breast."

"I think I can guess."

Mamadou sighed. "At last she came around. Her eyes opened, filled with tears. 'You have saved my life,' she said, her first words to me, 'all I have is yours.' Does anyone ever mean that? Maybe sometimes but it was then that I noticed the figurine and I reached for it. Oh, I cursed my greed, knew too that she had seen it. She smiled, but her face hardened. 'This you must buy,' she said, and she gave me the price."

Daniel remembered. "Too much for a trinket, not so much for a work of art." He looked again at the figurine, smooth and alone in his hand. He held it out to Mamadou. "Yet, gift or not, I can return it. I have had enough of its benefits."

Silence stole upon them, darkness too. Mamadou stood with his hands on his hips, his eyes downcast. He shook his head, "Who ever has enough of life? At first it is trivial, then quickly we see no vessel of adequate size to contain it. It overflows, fills other vessels and leaves them cracked and stained. We stand at last amongst the shards." He shuffled his feet on the rug by way of illustration. He then turned from Daniel and looked out the window at the sparkling city.

He resumed his discourse in a low voice, "What are we then? We become an empty vessel on a sticky mess. Maybe then we have had enough. Maybe then it is time to go." He glanced over his shoulder at Daniel, and then returned his gaze upon the city.

Daniel's own gaze did not travel so far; it stopped at Mamadou's balding pate. He saw beads of sweat gather there, waiting, anticipating. The figurine lay heavy in his hands, suggestive of imminent action. The shadows on the wall imitated the tableau being acted out. A sharp arm shot upwards, jerked downwards again and one shadow folded from sight. Some dark flecks spattered the wall where the shadow had been. Only one breath remained in the darkness.

From above we see Mamadou spreadeagled there, crucified on the remnants of his feast. His stare empties to the ceiling, a slight smile frozen on his face. A dark stain spreads through the scattered rice. A hand reaches down, places a smiling figurine upon his breast. Then, the last shadow leaves and only darkness remains.

Daniel hurried home, taking backstreets, scurrying through deserted arcades. He was giddy with paranoia. What if he was seen? Then again, his cunning whispered, how would he ever be connected with this crime? There were eyes in heaven he knew, blessing himself at the thought, but those eyes had slumbered these last few years, had they not? Surely now this sense of sundering could be reconciled. Surely now the stars could shine down in fondness on Daniel once again. He would begin to grow again, attach himself once more to all the tasks and virtues that once had made him whole. He would be reconciled with Hortense also. They would pass together into mellow middle age, become smiling and silver, watch the sun in its permanent setting bathe the cocoon of the all embracing city. Only rarely would he seek out his den, merely to allow himself a knowing smile at his folly, sitting there counting the dustspecks continuously falling.

These thoughts distracted him and he found himself in the crowded Plaza of the Blessed Virgin. There she was atop her globe, her body swaying inside her metal robes. Daniel stared, felt the hairs on his neck prickling. This could not be right. The Virgin was laughing, her lips parted in a sensual leer. One of her hands held the snake as before, the other – no, it was impossible – the other wielded a sword, raising it with grievous intent skywards. No, it couldn't be!

Daniel sensed a presence at his shoulder. An old woman was beside him, her wizened features racked with mirthless laughter. "You love her then? The whore of New Jerusalem."

He pushed past her, heard her cackle infiltrate the swarming traffic, the buzz and anger of pedestrians. It was like swimming in the dream of a sewer, the sheer awfulness sweeping him on somewhere past hope. Daniel swayed sweating, almost drunkenly to his door. He careened through the wrecked apartment and sought out his den.

All would be as it was before, he assured himself. Everything would fall back into place. He gained the comfort of his armchair, allowed the beating of his heart to subside, the sirens in his head fade to a slight sibilance. Yes, everything would be as before.

He allowed his eyes to wander across that old framed photograph taken at that fashionable bistro. Long forgotten, another photograph with Hortense all smiles and curves and he, so handsome and warm. His degree in the liberal arts still hung there, yellowed with age. Daniel let his eyes wander to the cabinet which was still open, along its empty shelves and coming to rest, at last, on the broadly smiling figurine.

ANCIENT WAYS

There is something of a mini melee of oiks, punks, Poles and innocent bystanders. Recriminations are shouted; a car horn blasts from the stalled traffic. A driver unwisely offers an opinion and is told where to put it. The night is damp but possibly clearing. The chill is that dead midland's chill unbroken by sea breezes or mountainy gusts. It is a cold that lies there and seeps.

I have a friend under one arm, perhaps under two. "The fuckers," I say. They agree. The fuckers.

Standing on a hilltop overlooking the Central Plain, I try out the camera on my mobile phone. Bryan and Eddie are silhouetted sloping upwards to the megalithic tombs. Mel is off somewhere to the west practising his invisibility. I am hungover and strangely ecstatic. We are walking in the footsteps of the ancients. There is something appropriate about this coming together of three wise men and I on this particular hill. It's all a bit garbled I suppose, and I let the wind in to clear my head.

Mel materialises at my shoulder.

"They certainly had the view," he says.

"Who?"

"The ancients," he says, slightly abashed.

"I'd say it was more pragmatic than romantic. Strategic mostly. I mean, whoever holds the high ground has the advantage. They can't be taken by surprise."

Mel is struggling to light a cigarette in the near gale that's blowing, furiously sparking his Cricket behind cupped hands. "Aye, true enough. The locals will still tell you that 'ye can't eat the scenery'; but they don't starve." A plume of smoke swirls violently around him. "Look at John Joe there, doubt that he'll ever die of sentiment."

In a field below, a farmer herds his sheep but without the requisite Border Collie. Instead he steers the flock with a battered red Cortina. Parking, stalking, barking the horn, and all the while the tiny flock stutters towards the lower field. As the car idles closer I see that the farmer is a young man, early twenties, with the window rolled down and a long bare arm tapping the beat to the car stereo.

"What is that?" I ask.

Mel cocks his head to one side. "You know farmers. Dire Straits probably."

Later, we're driving the spider's web of backroads that take us back to the main drag. Eddie's at the wheel, he and Bryan arguing the relative merits of Thin Lizzy and Led Zeppelin. Neil Young is howling on the stereo.

There's a pub in the town with all sorts of pans, storm lanterns and bric-a-brac hanging from the ceiling. There's a television high in one corner and a bookmakers next door. Eddie suggests we have a wager to keep company with the pints. There's a horse called Boot Hill running in the two thirty at Punchestown, and I figure that's an appropriate name. Nobody sees it. I put a fiver on the nose while the others pool their resources on a tip from the barman: some pantomime horse, a rocking horse. Bejasus they'll be out there tonight looking for him with flashlamps.

In the finishing straight we're neck and neck. We crane silently, awaiting the screen's benediction. Boot Hill is getting the edge. "Come on," I whisper. Then louder: "Go on you good thing you." Then: "Go on my son! Go on my son!" And Eddie looks at me strangely out of the silence of the trio.

I should say that these weekends away are a regular but infrequent occurrence. Once a year in the off season, the four of us pick some remote location with a sporting activity tacked on – a round of golf, a mountain hike, a fishing excursion; but this is not the essential ingredient. I suppose, in this allegedly enlightened age, the whole exercise would be seen as male bonding

"We're too old for that. Too old!"

Bryan is insistent. "Yes, but the young ones are mad for it these days. They'll even make the first move ..."

"Yeah, for the fucking door."

"No, really. You wouldn't believe the young ones hanging around the rugby club. Snobby little bitches, but man, they're gorgeous. Everything on show, and no bother checking them out. They'll egg you on."

"Maybe they're betting you'll get a coronary," I suggest.

"We're past it!" Eddie reiterates.

Bryan is not to be dissuaded. "They're not ageist. They're not like they were in our day. They're mature and they like maturity. Men improve with the years, you know. A good man is like a vintage wine."

"Or a mouldy cheese."

And so on. Such debate had developed into the alternative of doing. Could we still turn heads? Did we ever? Bryan goes to the toilet.

"Bryan seems to forget," I say, "that if women were vampires then he was our clove of garlic. Our very own woman-repellent."

Eddie laughs, though Mel is more exercised by the parallel between women and vampires. The analogy is extended, painfully, until Bryan returns whereupon it develops into personal accounts of the various vamps and goths we've known.

The goth would be mine, though I must keep quiet about certain details there. Ironically, that particular affair would precisely illustrate Bryan's point about these being sexually liberated times, with Ireland a honeypot for the ageing Lothario.

The goth's name was, incredibly, Odette. She hung out at the Harbour with a murder of crow-clad friends who were a fixture on the periphery of the music scene; not quite sneering at us 'boys' playing summer blues in the beer garden. Amongst them I recognised Maura, daughter of a friend of mine and a girl who could eat for Ireland. Maura was sweet, a chocolate soufflé, or a barm brack if you counted her many rings. Through her I got to know the black circle. The other scrawny kids were nameless and even blameless for a while. But Odette, she was so svelte, so poised, so elegant; especially when placed beside her plump and pierced familiar. And she was so young! Maybe only half my age, maybe even less and I was flattered, consoled even, that I had the presence to turn a young girl's head.

She told me she was sixteen when we fucked one summer's night in the boathouse. I was horrified. So horrified that I did it again, right there and then. What was it anyway? Sixteen, seventeen; who's counting? Autumn began the falling away. I had bad dreams about meeting her in her school uniform, all pigtails and freckles where before had been Cleopatra in mourning. It just wouldn't do.

In truth the whole thing faded. It was a phase I was going through, I guess, and I came to appreciate the adage that a man is as old as the woman he feels. Why fight it? Why revisit all that teenage angst? I could look forward into that descending tunnel, the glare of summer still strong on my back, and distantly discern a pinprick of light, silver and unmoving as the northern star.

So, I reconciled to my lot and contributed to the statistics. We had our two point five kids, or thereabouts: a boy and a girl, enough for replacement theory. The world ticked over. The others contributed their tuppence half-penny worth: Mel, two boys, Bryan two girls, Eddy a trio. We became four avid fathers, briefly reading signs of genius in the entrails consigned to the latest Pampers. Then we grew back to football and beer, and a fiver on the favourite.

I find myself outside in the unslanted drizzle talking to the Polish doorman. We share cigarettes and sulphur, moving on to compare notes on our loved ones. It's the same all over the world. His wife is pregnant and if it's a boy he will be called Patrick.

In honour of the saint?

He shrugs. A good Catholic name.

And if it's a girl?

Hmmm. Patricia!

Now, why do we find that so very funny?

The band takes to the stage and that's the end of that.

On our way back to the cottage Eddie puts on Pink Floyd. I think Money is playing but then sound and time seem to soften with distance. As we pull up outside the cottage at last, I listen for the heartbeat. There is a cold rush of air and I realise I am coming around from a daze in an empty car. I can see my friends silhouetted against the perimeter fence. They are pissing into the bushes. I join them. What's wrong with the john inside? I ask.

"Tradition," says Bryan.

There's a lot to be said for tradition. I let my eyes arc upwards in the silence and the steam. The Milky Way stretches like a bridge across the sky.

"Stars," I say.

"What is the stars," Mel says.

Bryan is inclined to be literal: "Millions and millions of gaseous balls."

Eddie laughs. "Gaseous balls, I've heard it all now."

"What do you see?" I ask him.

"Darkness." He lights up a joint. "It's mostly dark, as the song says. It's something like a light year on average between the stars. Six million million miles and mostly night for certain, just night."

He exhales into it and passes the joint. I smoke and the air grows cold. Bryan and Mel have turned back towards the cottage. We linger in silence for a bit and I pass it over again.

Eddie takes one last toke. "There's something I meant to say …" But then he coughs quietly.

"What?"

"Roached," he says, and flicks it into the bushes.

I did meet Odette again. It was at some gig and I had made my way to the bar to escape the sheer mayhem of it all. She was less the monochrome scarecrow of old, she was much less the opposite of old. She showed her blushes.

"Well, how's it going?" she asked.

It was going well. All's well that ends well, at least when it's over.

After a bit she took her drink and prepared to return to her friends. Then she stopped, half turned to look up at me.

"I was eighteen you know. Back then, I was eighteen at the time."

I told her I knew. I couldn't help it. People just lie, all the time. They lie.

Inside we never grow old. We carry a child around within us, from the cradle to the grave. It's our shell that hardens; wrinkling, coarsening, thickening. We're tough nuts, at the end we're really tough nuts. Inside.

Did I mention the band? I don't mean our own band, Mel and me. You know all you need to know there. But the band playing that night were the pits. Oh, we witnessed the sound check and god knows that was ominous – the deafening smack of the drums, the dead ringing chords and the counting. One-two, one-two; much too few numbers and way too much counting. We could have told them a thing or two, one-two, but there was a drink quota to be met and exceeded. After a brief oasis of calm the real thing was even worse. The first chord flattened everything within a mile radius including the beer.

What happened next remains a little vague but I remember a shouted conversation with the bassist punctuated by graphic expletives and significantly vulgar gestures. I was in form all right, they told me later. I mean, really, I had taken a barrel load of such crap in my time and anyone up there on the killing floor should have been well able for it. If you can't stand the heat ...

"If ye can't take the volume ye're too old, so take it outside!"

Outside was where we ended, eventually. It was as well I had earlier won over the Polish doorman since the opposition soon swelled beyond a four piece and suddenly sprang a fan base of a half dozen rowdy locals. They may not have known much about music but their scrapping skills seemed impressive enough in the warm up. By the time we made it to the frozen pavement some slaps had been landed but nothing serious. The narrow lobby and my Polish friend had also filtered the opposition down to something less daunting and with the dying heat the last missiles exchanged were verbal. The fuckers, aye, the fuckers.

At some godawful hour I'm crawling through a forest of deadmen, drooling and muttering. At the end of a long narrow room, much longer than I had remembered, sits Mel, side on to the fire. He's poised like Whistler's mother, eyes half open and snoring softly. I crawl through the damp and sticky undergrowth at the edge of the forest, undergrowth that resembles a carpet – or is it the other way round?

"Abawsh, jawabeen. Jowa bell?" I say, but Mel doesn't stir. "Abba jreem. Whach azba zeddy jreem."

Mel opens one eye to look at me. "That's easy for you to say," he says.

Stan was a friend of mine from schooldays. I say friend in the broadest meaning of the word. We knew each other and there was no particular dislike between us. In truth, I always thought that there was something vaguely unsavoury about him. I ran into him in my local some twenty years after I had last seen him. We recognised each other immediately, if a little warily. Over a pint he told me what he had been doing all those years. Working building sites in Britain and Holland, hanging around some, and a spell with a rock band, just like me. He had returned home, married, joined the fire brigade, all about ten years ago.

One day he was called out to a blaze in a four storey block near the city centre. It was his first major fire. "It was a fucking inferno, man," was how he put it. "Did you ever stand outside one of those things?" he asked. "I don't mean a house fire, which is bad enough, but a raging inferno. It's like a ripple passes through reality and you're changed, not just the burning building but everything you see and everything you feel inside. And the worst thing is that you want to be in the middle of it. You want to be inside the deafening crackle and noise."

I compared it to the iceberg. Two thirds of the iceberg is below the surface and it isn't silent. Eddie had passed near one on a cruise ship in Alaska and told me in breathless detail how it had crackled and roared.

Stan looked at me coldly. "It wasn't anything like an iceberg, man. It was a fucking inferno."

Stan was the man for a hot situation. On the top floor he had found himself isolated.

"They were calling for me, I could hear them even with all the crackling timbers. Fact is, I was looking for a way out when I tripped over this form at the top of the stairwell. I lifted him up and remember thinking how light he was, weightless. But he couldn't have been, he was a guy about our age, a big burly bloke. I was the one that was weightless. I was so up for it all, like being high on a drug. I carried that guy down three flights to safety. I was a hero, man, a fucking hero."

These things don't work out well, do they? You can tell from the shaking of the head, the look of sad experience. Stan became a haunted man.

"I had this local where I used to go alone. A bloke pub, The Railway Bar, you probably know it. I liked to go and do a few horses, or read the paper, chat with some of the guys I'd know. There were no firemen or family. I liked it. Well, your man traces me down. Not in a bad way, it's just that he wants to say thanks, like everyone does. Buy me a pint and pour out the gratitude, that type of thing. People always say they'll do it but they never do. People forget. But this guy didn't. And he didn't just want to tell me what a great guy I was, he wanted everyone to know. It was em-barrassing man."

In short, Stan had got himself a stalker. An amiable and upfront stalker, but a stalker nevertheless. The cheery face would now precede him to the pub, pints ready and a stream of praise prepared to flow loudly from his lips. Eventually, Stan had to forego his friendly local where everyone now knew him as a hero. The stalking fizzled out but not the feeling of being stalked. It was an abstract stalking; the feeling at any one time that, in doing what you do, you exercise a power of life or death over others. He reckoned he could deal with it, if he didn't dwell on it.

"It's a funny world," Stan said. "Sometimes I wish I'd left the fucker there on the stairs." He sipped his pint and smiled. "No, that's not true. That's not true at all."

I drift back to that secret Eddie told me in the rising smell. He told me of the serpent in the blood, that fluke of fate that had singled him out. And when he finished he leant closer and said, that deathless phrase: "Don't tell a soul."

I swore and I swore and I swore. I would take it to the grave, I said.

He reminded me that that was unlikely to be necessary. By then, all would be revealed.

"Unless you kill me now," I said.

Eddie laughed, which was something at least. "The thought had crossed my mind," he said.

We are speeding into the tunnel and we pull the tunnel with us as we go. We are four good old boys on the raz. Darkness shrinks before our headlights and swallows our tail. We are in the intestines of the beast and all around us is life. It glows like a ghost, skeletal and stark. We go on hard into the dark, and the dull rock beat builds higher and higher.

There must be some kind of way outta here
Said the joker to the thief ...

There is nothing else to hear but the distant whoosh of the disappeared lane and the thud of the speakers. Beyond the headlights all is dark. We can't see where it is we are going. We really can't.

CLOUD CITY

Dusk had yet to gather beyond the glass fronted entrance of Cloud City's bus terminal. There was a subtle deepening of the reflected sky in the facade of the art deco building and an imperceptible lessening of the afternoon's heat. Each passing minute stilled the dust devils on the pavement and thinned the scent of columbine in the already thinning air. As the Greyhound pulled away, five of the half dozen alighting passengers scattered like papers in its wake, but the other one stood still by the kerbside facing up the incline with calm expectation. Only as the scene settled to leave her in splendid isolation did she move, barely sigh, and finally allow a frown to cross her smooth features.

Hannah had been here before, but even then she had been struck by déjà vu. She knew the jagged mountains that rose beyond the town and the diaphanous towers that reflected the sky, blue and cloudy by day and black and twinkling by night. There were places up there on Main Street, she was sure, where she had drunk coffee and smoked Marlboros as the citizens of Cloud City passed aimlessly on the sidewalks. Or maybe before that she had floated on the raised boardwalks, all bustles and stays and swinging parasol while dangerous men tipped their hats on passing. Now she waited and her patience was rewarded with the approach of a low slung car.

The Chevrolet was in the classic mould with fins and grinning grilles, low and wide on the road. It would one day be made over as a desirable vintage, its owner proudly pounding on the wax, but this was not the day and Brett McTaggart was not that owner. It was not exactly ironic that McTaggart was Gaelic for son of the priest; he may have regarded religion as an abomination but he held such views with religious fervour. He was darkly attired too and dark and sombre of looks, his bristling hair and bristling beard prematurely flecked with grey. Hannah smiled to herself at a sudden insight. The son of a preacherman, she muttered beneath her breath.

Brett did not apologise for being late. He was worth waiting for, he was sure. He shook hands and chanced an awkward air kiss, then leant back, hands now safely pocketed and regarded her a bit too long for Hannah to be strictly comfortable.

"Well," he said, at last, in a practised western drawl, "don't you look good."

She was irritated. "I look better sitting down,"

Brett shrugged and opened the passenger door for her with an exaggerated flourish. "Is this all?" He addressed her bulky, but lonely, holdall.

"I travel light," she said, sitting in and slamming the door herself. Brett snatched at the bag without enough care, and was conscious of a hot twinge in his back as it thumped heavily into the trunk.

Hannah wanted to pass by the Silver Dollar, even to stop in briefly, although she was tired. Brett convinced her of her tiredness and she couldn't be bothered arguing. The

Chevrolet lumbered up Main Street. Its dusty windshield filled alternatively with buildings, wires and sky as it negotiated the tilted, undulating city grid. There was a no smoking sign on the dashboard which caught her sullen attention. It wasn't that she wanted to smoke; she rarely did when sober. But who the hell put a no smoking sign in their own car? Surely you would know the rules of your own car off by heart, especially if you were Brett McTaggart. At any rate, there was a smell of smoke in the car although that was more the smell of a diseased engine. It made her nauseous and she opened the window.

"Hot?" Brett asked and, in a show of sympathy, began to fiddle with the air conditioning which now released sporadic blasts of fetid fuel-soaked air into the compartment.

Hannah sighed. "Christ!" she said.

She consoled herself in the monotony of the street names, first, second and so on all the way up to twelfth where Brett swung recklessly left onto a wide avenue heading up towards the hills and into the sunset. She remembered the avenues with the houses detached and set back amongst the pines, indiscriminate in their mixture of culture and class. Great colonial piles stood beside modest timber bungalows while gothic fantasies were sandwiched between plain ticky-tacky. This eclectic mixture extended to the churches – Our Lady of Guadaloupe shining splendidly in the shadow of disapproval of the Free Baptist Hall of Reverend Zemeski. Leaving Osgood Avenue, they crossed the level crossing and turned onto Hutchinson Avenue where Hannah caught sight of the Silver Dollar, its neons just shimmering on and the sky behind burning with the electric dusk of some fantastic aquarium. She wondered if the boys were there.

Brett read her mind. "Don't figure on the boys being there," he said.

"Why? Don't they do the best Manhattan in Cloud City anymore?"

"I wouldn't know," Brett failed to elaborate.

"Maybe later we can check it out then," Hannah could feel her words fall without conviction.

Brett fumbled in his door and drew out a cd case. "I picked this up in Iceland."

Hannah wondered what you could pick up in Iceland. It seemed too clean. That being the reason why Brett had been there, she supposed – so clean, so white. Maybe you could catch alcoholism, but with a lot of determination. Brett put the cd in. It was Bjork or something similar. The rest of the journey was quiet tedium interspersed with unexpected shrieks.

Cloud City hadn't been long growing. The first clapboard shacks had sprung up in the yellow haze of the goldrush, populated by desperados who had come to dust the sharp mountains for loot. Speculators moved in and carved up the country into rectangular plots. Saloons and cantinas sprang up, the first rough hotels, casinos, a brothel or two and, of course, the Opera House. Then the more legitimate businessmen: bakers and bankers, lawyers and journalists. Deep down though, Cloud City remained a town of miners and whores, gunmen and gamblers, renegades attracted by the promise of golddust and held by the dirt of money. It all seems cleaner now, the financial district soaring and sparkling like a cold fairground, but still just a town of miners and whores.

Hannah found herself in Brett's yard, exhaling smoke savagely into the fallen evening and wondering how long it would take her to hike down to Main Street. It wasn't going well. She wished that the house on Elm Street had lived up to its billing in a more dramatically gothic way. Something a bit more turn of the century would have been fine, a mansard roofed turret and some shingle cladding perhaps, but instead it was sixties-ish anonymity with picture windows and featureless planes. She didn't quite feel that she had walked into Bate's Motel but something about the sober furnishings, more stealthy than comfortable, gave her the creeps.

Brett was the perfect gentleman, or at least a passable imitation of one. He rubbed his hands and bared his teeth in an attempt to convey joviality, or anticipation – she wasn't sure – then promptly began banging around the kitchen dismembering vegetables for the promised feast. There were vegetables she had never seen before, most still coated unpromisingly in mud and sprouting unhealthy explosions of leaves. Hannah had wondered whether he was preparing food for a herd of rabbits before realising beneath Brett's pitying stare that, no, this was to be their meal.

She had left him to it in the fluorescent glare of the kitchen, sweat and resentment shining on his skin, and gone out to the yard to light up. She thought that Brett would have had it all mapped out but that was true only insofar as things pertained to himself. She had forgotten how singular he was, how engaged he could be with his own charisma. There he was at home, if this really was his home and not the stage set of a reality-show or a safe-house in some witness protection programme. There was Brett at the centre of everything, in the kitchen preparing dinner which he would then cook, serve and wait for her to admire. And then what?

"You do remember?" she had to ask. "You do know what I'm here for?"

He made a dilettantish gesture while tossing the salad, "And here I am," he said.

She swore and turned away. "The past," she said, "but not *that* past."

She excused herself and said she needed time to freshen up, but mostly it was to stand still in the shower, thinking. The weightless spray bore her up and bore her backwards and, forming its dense mist, became for a moment the clouds that pressed down eternally on the city. In the whiteness she thought she could discern the drooping lattice work of telegraph wires, remembering how that gloom seeped into the interiors of the buildings – the hotel lobbies, saloons and even into the redbrick sailing ship of the Opera House. She had always wondered what that was doing there, all that finesse and frills amongst the shotgun shacks of Main Street and, within, its velour drapes and chandeliers an ironic riposte to the all-prevalent stink of tobacco and horse dung.

She wondered what *she* was doing there.

Hannah had come from the nothingness of Cloud City and now she was back again. She knew her family name was engraved on the rustic sign above the door of the Silver Dollar Saloon, a faded reminder of the days when it was known as D'Arcy's Bar. She knew old man D'Arcy had been a miner but where exactly he had come from it was hard to say. He was probably of Irish stock, but she had yet to find a satisfactory paper trail to link him to anywhere outside Cloud City.

Where exactly he had gone was something of a mystery too. All Hannah knew was that he had married the singer, Annie Oriole. They had lived a life of laughter and shrieks, punctuated by mutual left hooks in the tumble-down bar D'Arcy had bought with the silver he had scraped from the ground. She had left him with twin boys and a blue-eyed girl. Then left him for good and all, taking the golden arm of a suave Southerner who had massaged the card tables of bars and railcars all the way from the Great Plains to the Pacific. Oriole didn't quite disappear; she carved out a tawdry career of sorts in the dives of San Francisco, ultimately saved, in sentimental legend, by her blue eyed daughter, before this brief mythology itself faded.

D'Arcy himself had vanished as if a frozen cloud had floated down from the mountains and carried him off into the West. By which time Cloud City itself was sinking. Hollowed out of its silver and sodden with rain and snow, it was preparing to slowly rust back into the earth from which it had sprung. Yet it had survived, and the D'Arcys had survived, or one of them had.

The local priest, Father Daniel, had seen to their schooling but decided that the boys should be schooled separately. And so, ten years after, Bill D'Arcy received the benefits from the sale of the Silver Dollar and got a boarding school education with the Marist Fathers in Chicago. He was Big Bill D'Arcy in his college football days, and then a pugnacious journalist who made money and trouble in equal measure and who, on a sentimental whim, came to live in Ireland after the failure of his first marriage. That was how Hannah came to have a grandfather who was a Yank, after he somehow managed to marry into good Limerick Catholic stock, his money probably talking up an annulment and helping to suppress unwelcome gossip besides. That was the D'Arcys for you; blink too often and they're gone, or peculiarly changed.

It was the missing strands in her own old country, in America, that Brett was supposed to pursue and unravel for her. That nebulous first marriage, for instance. What became of Ted D'Arcy and the blue-eyed daughter, Annie? Where was her skin and blood now? Was there any there in the red clay beneath Cloud City?

At last Brett remembered that he knew how to show a gal a good time. He uncorked a bottle of wine and told her they would return to some of the old haunts which he figured might help. It was only white wine, she noted, but she was anxious to push the moment.

"Now," she said.

"The past," he replied.

"Yes, but *now*."

And so they took the Chevrolet down to the bright lights, through shifting curtains of mountain cloud. They continued on down Hutchinson to 13th Street and as they taxied up to the kerb outside the Silver Dollar it was clear that whatever bright lights had once been here had long since dimmed. Even so, through the murky air, she could make out the D'Arcy name still swinging there on the sign over the door. It was cold and the street was eerily deserted as they stepped onto the sidewalk. From the doorway beckoned the muffled sounds of the bar room, laughter, oaths and the tinkle of glasses. She was tempted but she demurred. She took out a cigarette and flicked her Mustang lighter. Brett coughed and indicated a plastic sign by the window. 'No smoking,' it said, 'within fifteen feet of this doorway.'

"Well, I won't go far so."

He smiled, for once.

"You go ahead," she said, "I'll take five."

Hannah slouched at the doorway, resting her ass on the sign. She had to hug herself it was so cold. It was misty too. It seemed to Hannah that Cloud City was being disassembled before her eyes. Looking off down deserted 13th Street the financial district had gone. In its place she could just discern the gaunt girders of the mine shaft and, closer, the railway line running unobscured towards the mountain pass.

She took one last drag, threw the butt into the muddy street. With an insistent heartbeat she recognised the footprint of Brett McTaggart frozen into the mud, then the fresher footprints of a larger man. Time pressed unexpectedly in on her and she turned and hurried through the saloon door. Inside there was a pregnant hush, and she could sense that all eyes had turned to her and away from some suspended drama. Through the smoke she saw the boys, Alvin, Rick, Leo and Chuck, together as always but strangely changed. They were both older and younger which somehow made sense, like the feeling you get from an old family photograph. Their chins were stubbled and their young moustaches drooped but, more than that, there was a sepia, old world patina to their clothes. Hannah realised that the wear and tear was genuine and not the factory stressing you would find on the racks at Sears.

Their eyes, and her's too, were drawn back to the drama and the giant figure of a man at the corner of the bar. A mighty grizzly bear of a man who turned and spat fire.

He sat with his back to the door, something he might usually have called careless, but it was complacency really, he liked that distinction. The saloon and its clientele soothed him, the lemon glow of the lanterns, the slow swirl of smoke about the rough timbered bar, the glow of liquor in bottles and glasses and, beyond the murmur of the card players, the whistle of the wind through the cracks in the door jam. Indeed Cloud City itself soothed him and that made a change. He was safe here except maybe in the frisson every so often of a quick glance from Jane behind the bar. He could take that as a hint of danger, or maybe the threat of more safety, but it didn't concern him much.

He held a dime novel on his lap and fell easily into the open pages. He would take the odd pull from the bottle of suds on the table, using the moment to cast his eyes about the room, casting them down again to avoid overlong contact with Jane's reciprocating glance. On the page Kit Carson was hunkered down in a dry gulch as five stealthy and murderous Cheyenne braves inched towards him. A tense tableau emerged from the abstract arrangement of words, so the comfortable interior where he sat warped itself into the wild yonder. There was a sudden furious burst out of the brush as a warrior charged with blood curdling shrieks and got to within six yards before Carson felled him with both barrels. But the exchange was enough of a distraction to allow the leading warrior get to within striking distance of Carson, his tomahawk lethally poised.

An adjustment of the winter wind outside and a sudden irregular beat on the boardwalk caused him to take his eyes from the page and shift in his chair to a position side on to the door. As if on cue the door swung blindly open, admitting a swirl of snowflakes and a figure clad in bristling black fur. It was soon obvious to those who looked that it bristled even more dangerously with energy beneath it. The sheriff knew who it was, casually marked the page with the Lucifer he'd been chewing and sat with apparent ease, his sheriff's star exposed and plainly shining.

D'Arcy had seen him but did not acknowledge him in his unhurried sweep to the bar where Jane was already uncorking a bottle and pouring a large Irish. This was downed in the growing silence, a silence emphasised by the snap of the empty tumbler on the counter. All eyes, the boys at their cards, Jane, the two strangers at the pushpenny table, were now turned to the sheriff. D'Arcy still loomed hugely but determinedly averted his gaze to a nothingness beyond the bar.

When D'Arcy spoke it was softly, but his words carried through the saloon. "There's them that are taken into this town to stop the thievin', and quickly turn into thieves themselves."

The sheriff slowly pushed the table back with his toe. "Welcome home, Jim," was all he said.

D'Arcy was pouring himself another shot, dispatched in the same manner as the first. "And there's some things that are stolen that you can never get back. Never."

That last 'never' was accompanied by the snap of the tumbler on the counter and once again the shift in the wind as the door swung open, this time admitting a woman they all knew, two of them too well.

A deeper gust of wind this time blew all the way into the centre of the saloon. The sheriff was aware of time slowing down in the fall of the snowflakes, in the cards rising magically into the air. He knew he was standing and he felt his knee bark off the edge of the table which pitched sideways and just hung there. In front of him the great bearlike shape of Jim D'Arcy turned and a barrel of metal gleamed out of the blackness of his clothes. The sheriff would have drawn too but Annie Oriole had moved into his line of sight. He shot out his right arm to push her roughly to the side when he heard the booming noise of the gun discharging, felt immediately the impossible stain of heat spread across the right side of his chest. The sheriff was catapulted backwards several feet into the drapes cloaking the front window. Only he could have heard the dull thud as he hit the frame which somehow didn't give but only slid him safely down onto the sill.

The ceiling was emerging out of the nothingness and peering down from it, at first a great ways off but slowly looming larger, were four friendly faces. He smiled and blinked with slow contentment. The boys, he thought, the good old boys. He heard Chuck's voice gabbling with excitement.

"I sure I done winged him, boss, but he's bigger 'n a bear and wouldn't fall. Done throw himself through the window into the alley there and take off to the mountains like a scalded grizzly..." Here, Chuck's narrative collapsed in a fit of laughter and coughing.

A friendly, older hand patted his shoulder, "You done good boy, real good." Alvin turned back to the stricken sheriff with more serious intent. "We can saddle up and hightail after him. Don't reckon D'Arcy'll get too far on that old roan of his."

The sheriff forced himself to sit up, pain shooting through his chest and shoulder. With difficulty he turned his head down to look at what should have been a blood shattered wound. He heard Alvin emit a low whistle.

"Don't reckon I've ever seen the like." The light of the oil lamp fell on the mangled parabola of the sheriffs badge. Alvin's voice continued with quiet awe. "Darn bullet must've just hit it and bounced. You're a lucky man, sheriff."

Then, at last, Annie Oriole's face came into his vision, a smile on her lips. "A very lucky man, indeed, Sheriff McTaggart."

When they helped the sheriff back to his chair, Leo put the novel back on the righted table. The pages were sodden with spilt liquor.

"Maybe you could put it by the stove for it to dry out, boss," he said, apologetically.

The sheriff shrugged. He knew the end to that story anyhow, it sang inside his head.

As the assassin paused the recognition dawned, Kit Carson saw that it was the old, familiar enemy. Black Bear realised he was discovered. Those Indian features seldom smiled. Maybe the mouth turned downwards that bit more. It was alright to be discovered now, as he prepared to dispatch his longtime foe. This was family business after all. Carson had married Black Bear's sister, Pale Star, a fact which had festered between them in the opposite of love. If this was to be the end after endless duels then it was worth savouring.

It was a fatal pause. As Black Bear prepared to swing his tomahawk, a shot skewered the air and he hung motionless, his eyes clearing and then glazing, before he pitched forward on top of Kit Carson. Carson was a survivor, but he would have struggled to believe he was still alive in the circumstances. He peered out from beneath the dead Indian to see that the three remaining assailants had scattered leaving only Pale Star standing there, all buckskin and beads with a Winchester lifted to her shoulder, one eye half closed.

CUPID'S STUNT

Sam Lyons liked his name, but that was because he had made it up. His own name, his own name … no, it was way too painful to contemplate. What had his parents been thinking? Well, he liked the name Sam Lyons and, you'd have to admit, it was a most suitable name for a sleuth. Oh, don't make me laugh, Sam the Sleuth – ha, ha, ha!

Look at Sam there, amongst the seafront throng, trying to fit in with his tourist's uniform. You know the gear - ankle length 'shorts', polo shirt, baseball hat and shades, all the way down to the Doctor Scholl sandals and Argyle socks. It's camouflage, of sorts, the way a zebra is camouflaged, a lone zebra. It's all so self-consciously real, like Sam is playing some entry level Where's Wally for us and we're going to spot him for sure. Eventually we will.

Right now it's Sam that's doing the spotting. Across the road from where he's parked in the tatty splendour of the amusement arcades, there's an oasis of sophistication. A paved terrace spreads before a cast iron porch, with potted cordylines and synthetic box, where the sparse clientele perch on patio furniture, taking their refreshments with tiny umbrellas and sliced, inappropriate fruit. Prominent amongst these, amongst the sophisticated clientele, that is, sit a couple poised in perfect equilibrium. So perfect, that Sam envies everything about them, except perhaps the fact that they're being watched by him. It is not that they are turned out the same, hewn from the same stone as it were, nor even that they are both beautiful, and they both are, at least across the softening distance. It is more to do with the poetry of the spaces between them, the way their clothes and hair flit in unison in the light sea breeze, the reciprocity of the rare exchanges between them. At least, they are the things that Sam is observing without necessarily comprehending in just such words. He is, nevertheless, acutely aware of that certain something.

He mutters under his breath as he reaches for his Canon, "Fuckers."

He has a burger in his car. It's an old seventies job, rust held together with izopon and packed with red leatherette and grease – the car that is, not the burger. Mind you, the burger's no great shakes either. Never buy a burger from an Italian. It's Sam's motto; but honoured more in the breach than in the observance. He just knows he shouldn't. What is it so? A morbid fascination like Russian roulette?

Sam remembers one of his first dates with Wendy. He wasn't as fat then, nor was Wendy. They weren't exactly a svelte couple, more like a couple of sleek sealions oiling their way along the rocky shore. She had asked him home that night which was the night of their third date. The first date had featured a chaste kiss, moving up to the second rounding off with some heavy petting in the Ford. The night ripened with promise at the invitation to come up: "for coffee, or something."

To celebrate, to build up the whole romance thing, to prolong the beguine, they stopped for burgers at Luciano's. Sam got a batterburger, surely one of cuisine's most sublime triumphs while Wendy was content with chips. They got to her terrace and Wendy made for the kitchen to put on the kettle.

"I'll put on some sounds," said Sam.

"Something romantic," she suggested.

He made his selection and Wendy, out in the fluorescent glare of the fitted kitchen was a bit surprised to hear the strains of Kung Fu Fighting by Carl Douglas. To be fair, Sam was a bit surprised too. He was taking his first bite of batterburger, through the golden warty skin of its exterior to its vaguely pink centre, (God's own supper!) and expecting to hear the music of Neil Diamond, that master of good taste. Unfortunately, some oaf had put the wrong disc into the sleeve and he was denied that subtle pleasure. In his distraction Sam inhaled and sent the first sizeable morsel of batterburger down the wrong tube.

He knew immediately something was wrong, all that exquisite taste bypassed and instead a feeling of inertia, a thwarted hiccough. He flapped across the living room gagging and croaking. As he thrashed into the kitchen, Wendy must have wondered at this strange mating ritual of her new boyfriend. Or was it that Sam was playing a frantic game of charades? It's a film, no, no, a play! Two words, first word, five syllables … sounds like, sounds like …

Everybody was kung fu fighting, sang Carl Douglas.

Wendy decided to play along and started to dance. She mimicked Sam's movement, trying to inject a knowing style into the jerky gestures, the frantic stomping. They approached each other across the tiles, like two rusted robots gone mad on rocket fuel.

Those kids were fast as lightning …

At last Wendy began to appreciate the problem. Nobody was that bad at dancing. Nobody had that complexion outside of the Blue Man Group.

In fact it was a little bit frightening, sang Carl.

In fact, it was very fucking frightening. Sam was convinced he was going to die to the theme of an inane Chinese riff and a one-hit-wonder. He sobbed and gurgled, and his legs began to sag. He was swimming in thick air as he sank beneath the ceiling to the tiled floor, far, far away. Suddenly Wendy swam past and he felt himself borne up by the oxters. To the independent observer, marooned by the stereo, resignation to Sam's fate was interrupted as the duo crashed back into the living room from the kitchen. Wendy had Sam gripped around the waist from behind as she struggled to perform the Heimlich manoeuvre on him. Despite his weight she was tossing him to and fro, his arms helplessly flailing the air. Push, she screamed, like a midwife at a violent birth. Push!

Waddling to the centre of the room, this strange composite shape paused for one last contraction and there was a gasp and a sudden whoosh as the sizeable first morsel of batterburger flew through the air and, amazingly, thankfully, struck the record arm and pushed it screeching into the spiral groove. Wendy flopped back onto the settee as Sam prostrated himself with gratitude and disbelief on the swirling carpet. So, the tableau of the would-be lovers was not, physically, all that different from what it might have been, and, with Sam lugging great bellyfuls of air down his scorched throat, there was even the throbbing percussion of heavy breathing. But all was still, and silence slowly descended.

"Thank God," said Wendy.

"Thank you," said Sam.

There was an ominous twist in the static and, behind their bruised eyelids, both knew that the record arm was jerking into motion again. The damn thing had been set to repeat.

There follows the telltale throb of xylophone as Carl Douglas winds up to give it all another go.

Everybody was ...

But the line was submerged beneath a barrage of oaths.

There is a picture of them strolling side by side, but not arm in arm, along the sunswept Esplanade. Mostly there are photos of them sitting together, close but not quite touching, at the more sophisticated stops along the seafront: the cafe bars and hotel terraces, that wine bar and the Italian place. These are not having much effect on the woman. Sam looks sideways at the unchanging expression, the cold skin pulled tight as a drum, the thin lips pursed and painted in an attempt to convey fullness. He thinks he sees the corner of her eyes flicker once, but this is just a nervous tic that repeats itself at irregular intervals and without apparent stimulus. She is a woman with issues, Sam decides, and a woman with absences.

The photographs are good, well made. Sam worked in the old fashioned way with negative film stock and had mastered his craft. He was a darkroom wizard but without any underhand trickery. Sam's photos didn't lie. They come to a shot showing the couple strolling the beach above the wave line eating ice cream cones.

Sam stabs at this and makes a satisfied grunt. "See," he says, then shrinks a bit as the woman turns a glazed look to him. "See, ice creams. That's significant."

The lips curl downwards. "They're eating ice creams," she says.

"Exactly," says Sam.

There is a short pause. "Fokking ice cream," she says at last, with appropriate iciness. "It's not exactly that they're eating each other."

Sam looks down at the ground. He wonders why a certain type of person, a certain class of person, preferred to leave the u out of fuck. Why? It just wasn't fucking without the u. It wasn't fucking at all!

They had reached another photo which he felt was even more of a clincher. Here, the couple both sat on the terrace, he with a broadsheet neatly open to his gaze while she was intent on a supplement or magazine, one eyebrow arched in frozen question.

"They're reading," Sam says, unnecessarily.

"I can see that," she hisses. "My husband is an intelligent man, Mister Lyons, and I can assure you that he reads extensively."

"But, they're both reading."

"And?" The woman arches her eyebrow in a manner that mirrored the woman in the photograph, but without the detached sense of amusement that the younger woman - and she was younger - showed.

"They're both reading, together." he says.

"So what?"

Sam is lost for words. He feels himself choking but it is choking on nothingness. The air has been sucked out of his universe and all the meaning scattered.

He grasps for something to cling to in the swirling nonsense. That final scenario swam past him again. They were both reading. They were both reading – together! Surely it was obvious.

"Are you all right, Mr Lyons?"

He nods.

An expression, not entirely unlike kindness, flits across the woman's features. "Mr Lyons, I do appreciate all the work you've put into this and, well, you can understand how it makes me look – through no fault of your own, I hasten to add – well, a bit silly ..."

Sam protests wordlessly, and she holds up a placating hand.

"Here, I had better fix up with you, I suppose, as we agreed." She snaps open her cheque book and begins to scratch out his fee, with a generous addition for expenses. "I suppose the whole thing should be a lesson to me," she continues, "and it just goes to show that life ..."

Sam's voice returns, but it can't manage more than a hoarse whisper.

"Sorry, what did you say?"

Sam clears his throat. "I said, just another one of Cupid's little stunts."

"Quite," she says, and hands over the cheque.

Wendy was cooking when Sam got home.

"What's for dinner?" he asked.

"I'm doing a fry," she said. "Thought I'd better use the sausages before their best before."

"Ah," he said.

"Eggs?" she asked, but was already cracking them into the pan without waiting for a reply.

"Easy over," he said and leant on the counter. It had been a hard day. The eggs sizzled in the pan and Wendy spooned the grease expertly, then looked up at him and smiled. He returned her smile with a broad, satisfied beam.

"What are you looking at?" she said and flipped each egg before returning her smile to Sam. "What are you looking at?" she repeated and they both began to laugh.

THE DUEL

I stepped off the edge of the world. I knew what I was doing. You know how it goes: you're living inside the bubble with no notion whether it's rising or falling, only the awareness of the confined space and the terrible transparency. So I picked the hotel for its remoteness, the sheer opacity of its hidden location and for its ill-defined extent – in other words the way that all those old hotels ramble not only through space but through time also. To make it all better on the day, the clouds were falling and the mist from the river valley was rising. The edge of the world, so, and the edge of another world meeting in tangent.

You can picture us arriving there, the heavy maroon Jaguar cutting furrows through the gravel, the cypresses standing sombre hard by the gothic exterior, off screen the tinkle of comfortable laughter. Or maybe that's larding it up a little. I drove a comfortable maroon sedan, a Ford Sierra which I had kept well, though it approached its use by date. I can't be sure of the cypresses but there were a lot of dark trees, diminishing to a faintly delineated end further up the valley. Gothic? Oh, I suppose, let's call it gothic for the fun of it all, and there was certainly laughter.

She is there, of course, all black hair and green eyes and unnecessary poise. In the car she had given the impression that she would sooner have been somewhere, anywhere, else, but now her diffidence has melted and she is ready to join in the whole charade.

"What is it then?," she asks, bright and breathless, "Are we Mr and Mrs Smith?"

I laugh, "Those were the bad old days."

"What then – Lady Chatterly and the Gamekeeper?"

"You wish."

"No, you wish," she says and turns a brief and insincere sulk back out to the endless valley. "Listen," she raises her hand in a dramatic gesture.

The silence seeps in around us, the cold and roaring silence. I try to focus into the nothingness and make a show of shivering as though that will coax her into revealing whatever's on her mind. "Nothing," I say. "And miles from no place, come on."

She turns back towards me and lets her hand fall onto my chest. "I know," she says, and then her eyes widen. "I know, I can be Dorothy and you can be, you can be," she pats my chest as the pause settles, then tippytoes to whisper in my ear: "The tin man."

"Thank you a lot," I say as I am left alone to swivel on the gravel, Dorothy brushing past on a scented wave.

She raises a beckoning finger, "Hurry, James, and fetch the bags."

There is a passage of time, the raddled ochre corridors, the severed antlers at reception, the oak stairwell, the flock wallpaper, the regency furniture, the fauvist prints, the diaphanous curtains onto the balcony, the plasma screen television. There is time to change our clothes and, once there, to perform an act of which the bishops, I believe, disapprove – publicly at least. I withdraw to the balcony and light up a pre-rolled joint of very good Lebanese.

Mysteries resolve themselves and I discern the fantastic silhouettes of castles, three, four and more, standing proud on overlooks still curtained by mist in the deepening valley.

"Look at this," I call. But Dorothy is off amid the tiles and flourescents of the en-suite, clicking her heels together and muttering something. I leave it a few minutes and call again, asking if she's ready yet. Eventually I have to knock on the door.

"Fuck off," she says, "and go to the bar, for God's sake." Still I wait. "I'll follow," she says at last.

The bar is a bit of a disappointment, to be honest. There's something very seventies-ish about it – deep leather armchairs and low slung tables. You can relax, sure, and drink too, but it is uncomfortable to do both at the same time. Nevertheless, I am happy. I smoke a slim panatella and beam contentment out towards the various small groups and couples scattered in the gloom of the bar's recesses. A giant screen shows a distant and irrelevant football match and is ignored, in so much as something so large and lurid can ever be truly ignored. I begin to fidget, I look at my watch and then over my shoulder where an inconvenient window reveals a small shard of the shrouded valley. I know – I'll take a pee.

I walk along a dark corridor to a single portholed door. I am reminded of a ship crossing we took once, long ago. You may not remember it well as you remained in the cabin while I walked the decks, amongst the living and the dead. I don't remember much myself, but there is a feeling that permeates the distance. It was the feeling that I was a speck poised above infinity, like a tiny spaceship on the event horizon, the sky subsumed in a gurgling black hole. Looking out at the malevolent ocean was bad enough, but down there in the corridors below decks was worse, the nothingness invisible and humming inside the metal and the bone.

Man, there was too much in that joint, it would be better to make it go further. I shut the portholed door behind me and rest against it a moment, eyes closed and skin cold and glistening. I become aware that I am not alone.

How can I describe him? He did not seem to belong to our age although he was not the only person I have seen whose dress sense was a bit adrift of current fashion. What was it then? There was about him something sepia and innocent, an openness of expression and stance that was not just essentially rural but also that little bit out of reach. In experiencing it, I was changing it, and yet I know I couldn't have changed it, not for the world.

His clothes were well made, of good material and impeccably clean. The cut was not particularly stylish, the grey tweed of the suit chunky in a manner that suited these hills, a warm, resilient material. I figured it was not new, but neither was it well worn. This was an occasional suit. He wore his flat cap with a self-conscious attempt at rakishness. This too was not a habitual item of wear. His dark hair pushed rebelliously out from beneath it, coarse, outdoor ploughboy's hair. His shirt was pastel and ironed, the tie toughly knotted, his brogues well polished and slightly worn.

I see him there, leaning slightly towards me, head inclined so he can scan me with one bright, suspicious eye. His hands hang loosely and there is the unusual thing, the one remarkable thing, really. He is carrying a soft case, a well worn leather case that I think, at first, is for a musical instrument. On closer examination, I see that it is a case for a hurley stick, and it's loaded. I nearly laugh. I have this peculiar vision of a prohibition gangster, you know, the sort you would see stepping from the black sedan and making for the doorway of the speakeasy, the grim violin case clutched underneath their arm.

I stop the laugh and, making space at the door for his exit, say lightly - "Up for the match, I suppose."

He considers this a moment. Swivels his head to scan me with the other eye. "I suppose? I suppose you could say that." Yet he makes no attempt to exit, and things become awkward again. The lights of the toilets are garish and one is not working properly. It flickers and hums and, as the silence stretches, this one, minor flaw begins to dominate.

"A local derby is it? Local sides, I mean."

He smiles. "It would be a matter of local pride, certainly."

I sidle past him to the stalls. Still he stands. Weirdo, I think, and his fucking hurley holder. "Are there many up for it, so? Just I don't see anyone in the bar or the lobby. Anyone in team colours, that is, or carrying gear." I clear my throat, aware that I'm rabbiting on. I unzip and release, relax a little bit, after all, this is what I'm here for. "Maybe you'll have time for a pint before the rest of the team get here."

"There won't be any drink before it, I can assure you, nor any parties intruding on it."

"Ah, I see." I do not see at all. I look over my shoulder at him. He is looking at me but at nothing in particular as though there is an audience just beyond me, expectant beyond the floodlights, looking up, waiting.

"It is between me and another party and there will be no one else with me, nor agin' me. It is a matter of honour, if you understand, and it is arranged to be so."

"So nobody will know, then?"

"Oh, it will be known. You can rest assured of that."

"And there's no other way of settling it?" I ask, because any brief illusion I had that this might be some sort of puc fada competition has been discarded. There's an undercurrent to his voice, a deep and bitter riptide. By now the fluorescent has deteriorated to the point that it is as if we are standing in strobelights. As I finish my business he has half opened the door, and he stands there, huge and proud, looking down at me.

"We know how to settle things. There is only one way and that is by facing the other party and fighting the wrong that has been done."

"But what is the wrong? Surely it can't be so bad…"

And he does a strange thing. He smiles, in a sweet but sad way, then withdraws through the door, closing it slowly behind him.

What could I do? I could hardly rip it open immediately and come after him. No. I allow a few seconds to elapse and leave the blinking, sizzling toilets for the gloom of the corridor. It is deserted. I sway along its length, back to the relative brightness of the bar where Dorothy awaits, impatiently.

The drink is an aperitif for a light lunch in the restaurant, an incongruous modern structure which juts out of the rear of the hotel, the floor to ceiling windows giving great views of the river valley. It is draughty, though, and the coolness pervades our conversation until we become aware that we are speaking in memos and soon stop speaking altogether.

Coffee appears and a thaw sets in. Dorothy asks for the evening menu and reads some excerpts aloud as though they were pithy comments in a book. To me it is all so much French buzz words, obscure cuts and fish, far too much fish. I have never bought into that whole culinary schtick. It's all fuel, pleasant fuel at times but fuel nonetheless. Still, it's good for a few reminders of times past: sneaking out of that restaurant without paying, the flambé that got a bit out of hand, the omelette from the dark lagoon. Oh, we could go on. I smile as Dorothy hysterically relives the end of another account.

"And then, and then the fucking eejit is waving his arm in the air and sets off the fire sprinklers. Hah! Oh, it was priceless."

"The look on his face," I say.

"The look on his face, oh, it was priceless." She pauses for air.

"Well, we won't know without trying."

"I suppose we're stuck with it, unless there's a few Egon Ronays up there in the mist." She knocks back her coffee dramatically. "That was piss."

I suggest a walk and she slumps.

"Do we have to?"

"Old times," I say.

The hike I've planned is easy enough. There's a good path by the river which then winds up through the woodland. Soon we're above the valley floor with silence seeping through the trees. As we climb higher, a muffled continuous sound grows through the quiet. The waterfall, I explain, and our walk takes a more ominous tinge.

The shelf in the valley, hewn by ancient glaciers, is poised between the rising mist of the waterfall and the falling mist from the mountains. The forest stands still. Above the trees the nearest of those fabulous structures I had noticed earlier is more defined and more prosaic. I had known they were the remains of the old tin mines, of course, exhausted and abandoned decades previously, but what the hell, I allowed the stone shafts and jutting girders to melt into gothic bastions and turrets. What difference does reality make to what you make inside your head? I find the mist eternally beautiful whether it's the breath of angels or the smoke of demons.

I emerge from a thick copse into a clearing with only the growing roar of the waterfall for company. There is a movement off to my left as if the flecked light and the shadows had gathered a shape to itself and stepped sideways. A small deer emerges just twelve feet distant and stops. She is a deep red and looks in my direction. She looks right through me then folds effortlessly back to nothing between two trees. I look around to see if Dorothy is there to verify the sighting, but she is not. I let go the breath I have been holding.

Dorothy is anxious to get back to the hotel. She complains of the approaching darkness, the constant damp and every turn on the way. She is certain that we will be lost and that somehow the deer, which she had not even seen, is a portent of this. We go straight to our room on returning and again we disrobe. The act we perform is certainly not discussed by the clergy though probably not unknown to them; we all talk to God in our own way. Again we shower, then dress for dinner.

You were never well disposed towards me at mealtime. It's probable that you found my table manners were lacking. You were probably right. They were always a bit, how should I put it, rough. I should be up there in my imagined castle eating game with my fists. Yet I feel I handled this meal quite well. I got through the soup without slurping while Dorothy expertly rifled the shells of several creatures of the deep. I deboned the fish with some panache, I thought, and resisted the temptation to order a side of chips. There was a dodgy moment over the wine where it took some persuasion to make me forego the red in favour of the white. I only relented when I felt that the waiter was going to cry.

You remember that time, I'm sure, in that posh restaurant down by the quays, where we sat with your posh friends drinking fine wine and eating rare meats. We had the best table by the huge stone hearth with a log fire blazing. Feargal, with typical aplomb, had the waiter place his bottle of red near the fireside and I, well oiled, requested the same treatment for ours. Except we were drinking white, of course. You were not amused, though your friends were, silently.

I tell the story to Dorothy who thinks it's a hoot.

"I was very young," I explain.

"That's not youth, that's idiocy!"

"I put it down to experience."

She raises an eyebrow. "Oh really. And what did you learn?"

"Not to drink white wine."

We raise our glasses.

The bar is busier now, the footballers on the screen more frenetic though no more noticed than before. Still, the noise of conversation rolls around the room as it would in a stadium. It's like a tide, that sound, at times distant and inexorable and then crashing in a violent muffled roar. I swim in and out of that vortex several times, the alcohol bearing me up like a lifebelt, smiling foolishly at the commotion.

Every so often I break for a joint, ricocheting along the furniture until I gain the cool and quiet of the car park. Few others venture out, thank God. It's too damp, too quiet. Have I been talking to anyone? I can't say for sure, but I feel I have been shouting or laughing for a long time. Then I find I have nothing prepared and must slalom back to the toilets again.

My head emerges from the sink and my features melt like liquid before reforming in the mirror. "Jesus Christ, Jesus Christ." I reach out my arms to hold the image steady and watch the greenish neon familiarity slip into place behind me. I breathe and turn and stand face to face with the man with the hurley. "Jesus Christ!"

He smiles at my shock and says "Pardon me" with that antique formality of his.

"What happened to you?" I ask.

He is much as he had left me this morning. The best bib and tucker may be a bit damp but still neatly arranged and I could say much the same about his curly black fringe. He is not wearing his cap which I notice is rolled and shoved into a jacket pocket. He still carries the hurley case. Down one side of his face from his hair parting to his earlobe and in extent not much smaller than a hand is a black carapace of dried blood. It is peculiarly isolated from his features and attire, only one stain behind his ear trickling away beneath his shirt collar.

"That particular matter which I might have told you of?" He phrases it as a question and I can only nod for him to continue. "The certain party has been dealt with, to our satisfaction, I might add."

I am still dumb. I point a finger at my own head, "But this," I manage to say, "you can't go about with that!"

He looks appraisingly at the mirror, even preens a little bit. "There would be little point in resolving the matter only to wipe away the record of it. There will be people awaiting my return, doubting Thomases if you will, eager to poke their fingers in my wounds."

I am nearly drawn to touch it myself. Instead I step back. "And what of the other party?"

For a second his look is sickeningly ominous, then it lightens. "You know what they say, about the other guy?"

I hear his laughter as I close my eyes and lean back against the wall. I let the laughter fade away to nothing before I open my eyes. I discover that I have a number prepared after all and follow the endless corridors back up to the open air. Dorothy will be wondering, but what the hell.

My joint-rolling skills haven't been improved with all the drink I've taken on board. I have assembled something that looks like an ice cream cone, and a half-eaten one at that. "Just one cornetto," I sing to myself and start to giggle, shuffling about the gravel car park looking for my balance. The top of the funnel seems hollow and I figure I must have emptied half the filling inside my breast pocket. What the hell. "Come here you little beaut," I say as I light it up and the top flares spectacularly, taking half my eyebrows with it.

As the glare subsides I see the surrounding trees throw their silhouettes like bones against a pulsing purple sky. For no apparent reason I am running and some vindictive force has sent the ground spinning up towards me. At the last second I dodge the impact by throwing myself sideways into the shrubbery. I lie there for a while. I realise at last that the joint is gone and a soft rain is falling. Bollocks anyway.

I could get used to this: lying on my back and looking up at the … at the what – the stars? The ceiling? It is all the one. Even here, on the threshold of oblivion, I see the twin arcs of Feargal's departing car swing across the curtains and recede with a rough edged hum. I hear your keys fumble in the lock. So, why is it that you can never make it home? And what exactly can I do about it?

Do I walk out there into the presence of the two glowing lamps? Wrench open the door and drag you out by the hair? Or perhaps I would wait until one of those awful art soirees, or theatre nights, where I know you and he will be present. I will walk up to him and, with suitable haughtiness, call him out for a duel. Oh, everything will be perfect, the trees stark in the frosted parkland, no one else but our shivering seconds.

Eventually I make it back to the bar. Dorothy is not impressed. The bar is really hopping now and above it all the giant screen glows, a fluorescent bowl of footballing gauchos pressing against its skin. Still I hear Dorothy whisper.

"You're drunk."

It is impossible to deny. My dishevelled state has drawn the amused glances of others in the bar. My shoulders shake with suppressed laughter. "You should see ..." I say, "You should see the other guy."

There is a long silence which is really impossible in this vortex. I hear Dorothy say, beneath her breath, "There is no other guy, there never was another guy."

Later, we negotiate the stairs and the corridor. It is a comradely three legged race accompanied by much laughing and swearing. In the sanctuary of the room we perform an act synonymous with the clergy, though generally thought to be denied them. Outside the wind is blowing and I fancy all the mist must be stripped from the valley leaving something stark and knowable in its wake. We lie side by side and hold hands in the dark.

"There's no place like home," she says.

"I know," I say.

"There's no place like home," she says.

I close my eyes. I see a meadow suspended over a sleeping valley. A couple emerge over the horizon, a man and a boy. The man is stocky and bald, his shirtsleeves rolled up. The boy is familiar. Both carry hurleys, the older man with a grace that belies his build. They pass across the field with purposeful strides and disappear again from my sight. Sometime later the sounds carry to me, a series of intermittent thwacks that soften with the distance and fade.

ONE FOR THE ROAD

The road opens outward like a book. Trees bend downward to the tarmac in dripping prayer. Heat rises to a louring heaven. The road is empty; the trees are full, pregnant. You are aware of the heat, aware of a sultry song lazily twanged.

A car emerges onto the road and buzzes with leaden determination towards the horizon. It doesn't sound too healthy. It is a sick car. Inside, the dashboard hums agreeably. Sinatra sings of somewhere beyond the sea. The driver taps the wheel and hums. He is offkey and tuneless, but he is smiling. He is overdressed in a manner not quite in keeping with these times. Retro chic, perhaps, you can't really tell. But it's strange, as though he has stepped out from a song, maybe a song playing on this radio, on an oldies show. There is the homburg, the blue double breasted business suit with the shoulders too broad, the black leather shoes tapping the pedals.

He is smoking low tar cigarettes. Listen. Hear that slight wheeze as he exhales? Tell tale sign, tell tale sign. You'll hear it in his voice as he speaks and you will put it down to experience. Somehow, you will believe him more.

When you travel that road you notice that the earth imitates the heavens, but poorly. The land is flat and black and the house lights are sprinkled like stars across meaningless distances. One thing the earth does well, excessively well, is neon. Neon is the supernova of imitation and it even extends to an imitation of that other life, the life within the lights that we fondly call the real world. There, a neon woman teeters beneath a gigantic ice cream. There, a cocktail glass rises hugely into the night, tipping its liquid in one undulating strip of glowing gas. Life is like that, you think, or wish.

To return to the man. Did you follow him in, incidentally, or was it just coincidence? The tarmac is chequered with large, dark vehicles. The landscape windows are screened by Venetian blinds. A jazz piano leaks notes through the doorway. You enter and take a seat by a window. You order a Blue Lagoon from the girl and wait for the approach. What will it be this time? All hairoil and shades or a crumpled suit and a lifetime passing through nameless cities selling consumer scurf to people they had seen in a mirror somewhere. No, it has to be him.

Cut forward, then. A lady, a brunette with high cheekbones and sleep-lidded eyes takes a light of her menthol cigarette from a man who has his back to the room. He has set his homburg on the table. His hair is oiled, old-fashioned, and his shoulders are broad. He is stuck there for the night, his car having its innards rearranged at some dubious garage nearby. She laughs softly at several things he says in a way that is deliberate, practised even. The night tumbles on. The time comes for him to tell his story.

In this story the man has a friend. His name doesn't matter. He is a man who is, somehow, irresistible to women, which is just as well as he has a voracious appetite for love. We all have friends like that - high achievers, charmers; we count ourselves lucky to have them. Still, we suspect that there is something missing in their lives; they have it too easy in that so difficult of disciplines.

The man continues his tale.

"It is not just that he is a hit with the ladies, you understand; they really love him. Whether it is a one night stand or a more longterm relationship, although longterm might count only in weeks for him, the parting is always always more fraught for them. There are scenes. Tears in the restaurant over the dessert trolley, pathetic wrestling matches as he leaves one more apartment, phonecalls at work, embarrassing in their entreaties, their persistence, before finally they fade. Yet he handles all that element of it, the messy endgame, with aplomb.

"He is unruffled by it all because the thing is, the thing that is missing is, that he has no feelings for them, no deep feelings. Oh, he appreciates them, compliments them, is lavish with the language of adoration. He's a good lover too, considerate, even clairvoyant in those details. Well, you know what I mean. More than that, he remembers the little things, dates and gifts, the minutiae of the stories they tell him. And he never lies, never two times them, but when the time comes, when the time comes - he goes."

The man extinguishes his cigarette and raises a finger for the girl. She attends the table and smiles. He raises an eyebrow at you and you incline your head. He makes an inclusive, stirring motion with his finger pointed downwards, then nods, emphatically, at the girl. She smiles again and says: "Certainly, sir." He resumes his story.

"He is a travelling man, like me, so I suppose a certain resistance sets in against the notion of settling down. Also, the world is your oyster. I mean," he laughs, "there are a lot of beautiful women out there and no law, of man or nature, that says there must be some kind of limit, that says thus far can you go but no further. It's a long road, as the song says: a long and winding road."

It occurs to you to continue: "That leads to your door."

"Sorry?"

"The long and winding road," you say, "it leads to your door."

"My door?"

You are amused by his cartoon obtuseness. It leads to a door. There is only one door.

He makes a sound between a laugh and an exclamation mark. "Yes, yes, it's just so, but I'll come to that. Yes, that is the point. First of all, though, there is the quest. My friend is searching - but for what? Like I said, there are a lot of beautiful women out there but my friend isn't a talent scout. Uh no. He told me once, when we were young, that he preferred dimmer girls, the dumb blonde syndrome, I suppose. But that, he later admitted, was only his own stupidity, his own ignorance really. Not that there's anything wrong with dumb girls; it's just wrong to set those arbitrary preferences, to set limits, to be closed."

The drinks arrive, a Blue Lagoon and a Scotch on the rocks. He pays the girl and tips generously. He raises his glass and you reciprocate. "Love on the rocks", he says.

"Or something", you say.

"Waitresses", he says, "can be airheads or rocket scientists, aspiring actresses or failed singers. Their glasses might be half full with history and hope or half empty with broken promises and disappointment. So, preconceptions can be stillborn, limiting. My friend has been to the five continents, across the seven seas. He's stroked the dark skin of a South Sea Island girl, cradled the blond head of a Swedish schoolteacher, shared the studio of a Roman sculptress, rubbed noses with an Inuit scientist. All different but, in the end, all the same. Though he tried he couldn't find any love growing within him. However much he enjoyed their company or the exotic tang of their location - he could never get that spark."

As if by way of illustration he lights two cigarettes with his Zippo lighter, handing the first to you. It makes you smile. Corny but smooth.

"So, there he is, without the spark without the flame and yet it seems as if he can pick any woman in the world. But where is she? Where is the one? Where does that highway go to?

"At last he comes to France. There is a job in Paris and it is a place he has never really been before. The odd tourist stopover, sure, the Eiffel Tower and the Arc de Triomphe, but never really explored, if you know what I mean. He realises too that Paris is the capital of the heart and that if he is ever to fall in love then surely it would be here. His sojourn in Paris is for a month and he has plenty of time to walk around and, surely, there is no better city to walk around. He takes a place near the Place de la Bastille and from there he can reach the Botanical Gardens and west along the Seine zigzagging between narrow streets and boulevards. The names drop like water, Saint Germain, Notre Dame, the Pantheon. He adopts favourite cafes and bars where he can sit and observe the people walking past, but chiefly, of course, the girls.

"On his second week he sees her. Quintessentially French, dressed in navy sailor's jacket, hooped jersey, black leggings. She has long dark hair, high cheekbones and her lips are held in a permanent pout. The works. The real thing though is this: though she returns his gaze brazenly there was nothing else to it. It is the same gaze she turns on anyone who looks, it is indifferent.

"This was just what my friend was looking for. A challenge. He rises to it too. He knows how to flirt, then how to court. He takes his time and even extends the time he must stay in Paris. Well, Paris is worth an extra month. Or two. They move through the different levels until reaching the physical, and that too is perfect.

"She works in advertising and lives in a small, tasteful apartment looking westward over the rooftops of Saint Michel, the Eiffel Tower in the background. She is a ti-gress in the bedroom, an artist in the kitchen and an en-chanting and witty companion at the sidewalk cafes they frequent. She can speak English charmingly, but he prefers when she lapses into French. He hardly under-stands a word but it is, after all, the language of love. Summer melts into autumn and then autumn grows cold-er as it falls towards winter. Everything is perfect and, one bright October morning he realises that he is in love. It had snuck up on him and taken him unawares, but there was no doubt what it was. Perfection. But for one little thing."

The man lays his cigarette carefully in the ashtray. The smoke makes a steady stream to the ceiling entwined with the dying smoke of its companion, the white French filter tinged with lipstick.

The man resumes. "So my friend, he takes a chair to the window and sits down and broods. At last his lover stirs and asks him if he is okay. He shakes his head and turns to explain to her. What can you say? What can any-one say in those situations? It's not you it's me. It's not me it's you. There is someone else. There is no one else. He had been through it so many times and yet he would insist that this once was truly unique. It was truly unique be-cause he knew that he was in love and it was truly unique in that she was not in love with him. The tables had been turned.

He remembers the silence into which his words fell. He remembers her ashen complexion. He remembers that it is already winter as he stands in the silence and walks, a man in a trance, towards the door.

Well, I suppose it would be true that he hoped, hoped more than expected, that she would do something to restrain him. He reaches the door and turns the handle. Nothing. He opens the door into the draughty stairwell, just a flight up from the lobby which leaks in the October elements. He stands there in the sharp cold, thinks of the swirling snow beyond. At last she calls to him and extinguishes all hope. Those parting words will always haunt him.

"Shut that door," she cries, "shut that door." What a fool he had been to think that love could be reciprocated."

You are still smiling the following morning as you make your way across the near empty car park. Yes, what a fool. You allow the early heat time to get out of the car, leaning against the door and looking down beyond the motel towards the lake and the mountains beyond. Sitting into the smell of leather you realise how new everything is. You check your mirrors and pull out onto the road.

The road is rising now between forests of uniform pine, thick boled and evenly spaced. The window winds down as the strains of the radio rise. It's some smoochie, suit music, some singer pining for the sea. You imagine the scene from above, the car tracing a dart of colour on the sinuous tarmac. The trees are laid out parallel, diagonal lines stretching forever to a billowing horizon. You travel up, and up. Clouds interpose, also arranged along the same straight, diagonal lines. There is no horizon for them to meet. At some point the clouds, their shadows and the trees form a moiré effect which is continuous in all four visible dimensions. It covers everything, effortlessly, continuously.

KINGS ON THE ROOF

Fitz was destined to be a union man. Sharp red hair standing in shocked homage to Karl Marx, aggressively bearded from his late teens, small and pugnacious. Unlike some I could mention, that distinctive Dublin patois was neither repressed nor enhanced; it was the real thing delivered without affectation, without apology. Socialism was hardwired to his soul, if you pardon the contradiction. I daresay he acquired the Leftist creed from a different pulpit than I. For me it was an intellectual exercise, the logical resolution of a set of moral and ethical issues. Fitz came up through the school of hard knocks, not something he was behind himself in stating. "Me parents had nothing; me grandparents had less," was a maxim I heard more than once.

We partnered on the southeastern maintenance route, from Dublin's leafy suburbia to the Wicklow uplands, spending long times in a van that needed to be filled with conversation, most of it his. I happened to remark once on the solidarity shown our brothers during a rare industrial dispute. It may have been from the Trinity Trotskyists, or was it Maoists, not that it mattered much. Fitz was unimpressed. "Students? What would they know of solidarity? Four short years in their aunt's Ballsbridge apartment, a degree conferred through cogging, ghostwriting and pull, followed by a round the world binge. Then home to P and M, and if the folks can't wrangle a job in the real world they'll let 'em park their arse in a top floor office at Daddy's company, in perpetuity. Bloody students."

Silence would ensue. I might mutter some tepid defense, only to draw the legendary ire on myself. Gimlet eyes would swivel from the road to fix themselves on my profile. The low growl stealing over: "There you are, a youth in training. Youth in training! With your Clint Eastwood boots, your Doctor Who scarf and your, your ... duffel coat."

Oddly enough, I've happy memories of my three or four months with Fitz. There was a purity to him, the saintly fire of the monk or martyr which, don't laugh, I found almost inspiring. Oh, I'd bigger ambitions than being a youth in training, much bigger ambitions than the fiddling of the journeyman techno or sinecured state servant. I was not so foolish as to share my ambitions with Fitz, but I reckon he knew anyhow. The Doctor Who scarf did it, and the cowboy boots. I resolved to ditch the duffel coat.

But enough of me. This story doesn't concern me. I heard it from Alex Leharte, the Albino as some called him. He wasn't, by the way, just had lank blond hair and a complexion that defied the caress of such sparse sunshine that fell on our dear isle. The Skull of Sheriff Street was another moniker, equally descriptive. I worked with Alex in the Sorting Office where we formed part, not a very important part, of the Engineering staff, maintenance division. This was after I had finished my training becoming, as it turned out, my last stop before leaving the service. Bigger fish to fry, bigger fish.

Alex remained a friend, of sorts, and we used to meet every month or so at Clery's Bar in Amiens Street, its gilded frontage parked discreetly under the railway bridge. It was a place of burnished conversation, focus slipping in the chamfered mirrors, groups huddled within swirling clouds of smoke, whispered conversations drowned with regularity by passing trains.

Alex would drink Guinness; myself Harp. I was a couple of years or so out of the service and the old days arose as a usual topic of conversation. The old days and the old stock. I mentioned Fitz as I knew Alex had worked with him too. Also, like me, Fitz had used the Sorting Office as an exit door not long after I left.

"Couldn't credit it," I said. "Always thought he'd see it through to the pension. A company man. Yet he bins it, mid career."

"I have my suspicions," Alex muttered.

"Can't be," I said. "Fitz was straight as a die. Must have crossed someone. Why else would he land at the Sorting Office."

"Not at all. Fitz was happy to be there. Happy to be off the road. Remember, he was second in command, with all that audience to proselytise. In his element, he was. No, there was something happened and," Alex made a theatrical show of glancing over each shoulder as though the denizens of the bar were hanging on our every word, "I've a notion what might have gone down."

It helps to share a past when you share such stories. Alex takes us back to the Sorting Office in a blink. From ground floor to roof, six floors above, there twists and twines a system of chain belts and chutes, ceaselessly carrying parcels of mail to wherever it is they're supposed to go. Imagine the sacks passing above like so many trussed up bodies. They come in, are dissected, rearranged, then go out again, sorted.

The word 'ceaselessly' back there is really to do with intent. Perpetual motion is achieved by perfect machinery, maintained by perfect staff. The system was not perfect; within its intestines tubes frayed, heartbeats faltered, electricity shorted and snapped. The staff were only human.

Clearing baggage blocks occupied a good proportion of the maintenance life. An occasional engineering gem might intrude, the plug of a kettle might need rewiring, a neon tube need replacing, but basically for us giants of electrical engineering it was baggage blocks and cigarette breaks. For the workers on the floor, the cigarette breaks came when we were clearing blockages. If the blockage could be organised just so, there might even be a chance to skip across the road to early openers like the North Star. Needless to say, clearing the blockages was easier than extracting the floor staff from the boozer.

"So," Alex went on, "I was on this morning with Fitz, relieving the previous shift which was Tommy Tighe and the Bishop. That night, Tommy was suffering with the nerves big time so, when a call came down from the Parcel Room at four am, he sent the Bishop to deal with it."

I nodded in a combination of disbelief and comprehension. The Bishop was a hippy like me but more full time, if you know what I mean. He got his name from an item in his flamboyant wardrobe: a purple lined coat that was, well, episcopal. He liked to take his smoking breaks alone on the roof, spending the time between breaks sleeping or glowering at the world from beneath half closed lids. Tommy was the senior man and, technically, should not have sent the Bishop off unaccompanied into the bowels of the Sorting Office. Then again, it was only a blockage; you could train a chimp to do it. Training the Bishop was a different matter.

"Funny thing about Tommy," I reminisced. "Always by the book till it came to the night shift. Used to head down to the Boiler Room where he could meditate or chant. Christ, put your heart crosswise sometimes. Once, he sent me off on a blockage up in the Letter Room. Man, those monkeys up there, they slung the bag over the hook alright. Fair enough, buy some time in the North Star for a quick one. You know what they did too, though? Bastards greased the railings where they knew I had to vault on to the gantry. I'm put into orbit like Eddie the Eagle, practically broke my snot ..."

At this point a train passed over, its rumble drowning the noise of the pub, setting up a charming tinkle of whiskey bottles by way of accompaniment. The lights flickered in a premonition of death. Alex's face loomed closer when it passed.

"Are you fuckin' listening or what? I'm telling a story here." The ambience had resettled into its familiar fraught conviviality. Alex took a long pull on his pint, leaving a white mustache on his ghostly face.

I laughed. "Right, you were saying, the Bishop..."

"The Bishop thought every day was Christmas, so this was something special. Of course, the Parcel Room was empty, nothing there but the rising sun and a stray rat. And, of course, a lone sack slung over a hook. The Bishop has to crawl up a chute to get at it. Course, when he unhooks the bag, this being the Bishop, he forgets that he's on a polished chute and, now being heavier with a full sack in his arms, he finds himself sliding downwards, as Newton might have predicted. The chute in question, the Helter Skelter, ran the whole way down to the ground floor. So, twelve stone of well oiled hippy becomes something of a howling blur, until he is ejaculated from the chute into the skip in the dispatch yard."

We laughed good and hard at that. The visuals evoked, indelible, irresistible.

"Ah, the Bish," I said. "You know how he got that name?"

Alex looked at me. "It was his name, you spanner. Mike Bishop."

"It was?" I examined the dregs of my pint. "What about the cloak?"

"What fucking cloak? Anyway, listen. The thing is that when he hit base, if you follow, the bag had come open and one of the parcels within, here we'll have to take the Bishop's word for it, had somehow burst, spilling its contents onto our friend's lap."

I emitted a low whistle and allowed Alex to take a long, last draught before interjecting, "Your twist."

Alex called a girl. He placed the order while scanning her body for aesthetic contours. "So, now the Bishop is the Santa Claus, because the parcel is packed with treasure. Gold jewellery, precious stones, fabulous watches with a bit of both, I suppose. The whole shebang.

"Now, as you know, this should have been reported but, as you also know, not every spillage is processed through the lost and found. There's a certain ... 'percentage'. I suppose that's the word for it. I mean, it's not that we're overpaid or anything like that. Be that as it may, finds like that are a bit big to stick up your jumper. There's a difference between pilferage and larceny, but such distinctions are low on the Bishop's radar.

"Also, there's no guidance from Tommy Tighe. In fact, sitting in that skip, covered in treasure, all the Bishop might hear of Tommy was low moaning chants coming from the Boiler Room – 'Om mani padme hum'. Maybe you'd have Jimmy the boiler man throwing in a few bars of 'We're on the One Road', if he wasn't sucking on a bottle. The Bishop, in short, is left to his own devices. Thinking like the devoted drugee he is, he decides to hide his stash. What better place to hide it than the gas oven in the staff canteen?"

I told Alex I could think of a dozen better places, a view with which he obviously concurred. The drinks arrived, Alex paying with a combination of pain and panache. Taking time for a slug of his pint, he continued his tale.

"The Bish, if you remember, was a vegetarian. Tommy was a vegetarian. Hell, even I was going through a vegetarian phase just then. The other half of the shift was on a maintenance course in the annex and so weren't expected for our dining pleasure. Ergo, from his perspective, the oven looked a good bet. As it turned out, no sooner had he put the stash there than he took some me-time on the roof, lighting up a spliff the size of an ice cream cone, promptly short-circuiting his memory in the process. When me and Fitz arrived, there was only Tommy, looking no more glassy-eyed than usual, standing there in that subtle tone of lurid orange he loved, giving us blessings like a noddy dog. It wasn't till our first break of the morning that events unfolded, as it were."

There's a rumbling off in the distance, an imperceptible dimming of the lights. "Fitz went across Amiens Street to his favourite butchers, got the usual haul of grizzly totems he called breakfast. You know the stuff, kidneys and gizzards and what nots. He liked showing me the contents, especially during my vegetarian phase."

Alex merged into an impression of Fitz. "'Look what I've got, Lexy. Look, nutty gizzards!'" He paused for another pull at his pint. "Nutty gizzards. The red head of him creased in that cackle of his. A terrible man. Thing is, now the oven was brought into play, cos that's where they kept the frying pan."

The rumbling grew closer and the bar began to oscillate at its extremities. Lights swayed and stalled, bottles jingled behind the bar, while the giant mirrors rippled, sending their reflections into a time warp. I looked at the pulsing ceiling. "Goods train."

"NET train, I reckon," Alex said. There was brief darkness before the lights burst ghostly again on the Albino's features. The trundling train receded. "There's Fitz, if you can imagine, looking not into a lake of yesterday's lard but instead Aladdin's cave. Oh, the shine of that jewellery, man, the shine. Well, you can only eyeball beauty so long before the cost begins to register. Fitz has gone white. He turns to me. 'You know what this is, don't you?' he whispers. 'No,' I said, 'no idea, no way!' 'It's a plant,' says he, 'those bastards on the top floor think they'll fix us up good.' You know Fitz, always giving it yards, how the top brass were out to get the union man, the working man, the man whose parents had nothing, his grandparents less. You'd want to see his eyes searching the room, for hidden cameras or what, I don't know. Every time I opened my mouth, Fitz would put a finger to his lips until finally he went into a mad dance, scooped the treasure into a bin liner, made for the door but turned to buttonhole me. 'I've got it,' says he, 'I know how to get it back to them.' Then he was gone."

A silence hung in the air and I was drawn into a response. "So he brought the stuff back, well and good. If you're not the Bishop, that is."

"Ah," said Alex, "not so sure. He could have said: I know how to get back at them; which has different connotations. Fact is, Fitz reacted quicker than I did. The Bishop was, as usual, sanguine enough: 'I'm not a breadhead, man,' you know the shit. If Fitz absconded with the treasure, who, exactly was going to say anything about it?"

"Well, the boys in the top floor."

Alex looked at me pityingly. "Conspiracy my arse. Maybe Fitz believed that or maybe it was just a ruse. Christ, there were no cameras or mikes. The only people who might tell were the Bishop and yours truly. Is that going to stand up in a court of law? Fact is, within a month, he was gone. Sold up, moved out. Living it up on the Costa del Something. Fitz, international man of mystery."

I had to admit it was a solid theory. But Fitz? Straight as a die. Part of the union. Much as I detest all that sentimentality concerning honour, honesty, sympathy with one's fellow man and all that, I still felt a pang of disappointment, as if a piece of me was dying. Still, what are memories but gilded imperfections? We must fashion some consolation from all the gold we've grappled for and lost. The truth remains poor; only the rich man enters the kingdom of heaven.

There was a time back then when everything seemed possible, even there in the Sorting Office, in the bowels of that clanking beast, amongst the trolls and elves of the workaday world. We'd climb onto the high gantry and up the fixed ladder to the roof, Alex, the Bishop and I. We were kings of the world up there, with Dublin spread out beneath us, above us only a rippling sky. I recall talking a good future then, fueled on hope, weed and like-minded friends.

The music is loud in my head as I point out heaven to my friends, tell them that's where I'm bound. Alex nods in agreement as the Bishop reclines against the ventilator shaft. He hands me the remainder of the joint.

"You know how he got his name, don't you?" Alex says.

"The Bish?"

"Yeah. Seems he was out here a year or so back, out of his gourd. So there he lies, in that perfect stillness so typical of the man." Here, Alex gestures and, true enough, the Bishop is indeed an admirable example of serenity. "When, who should arise into the plain air, only the anointed one himself."

"Eddie?"

"The boss fellow. Not only, but also, in tow, two engineers of high breeding. Seems our esteemed leader was giving a tour to the top brass, so impressive they adjourned to this castle in the sky. That sense of achievement, of perfection, was somewhat marred by our hippy friend sending up z signs in the middle of the working day. But Eddie is no slouch, he tells the others that the Bishop not only worked long hours but, born of a deep religious conviction, spent his nights working for the poor and homeless of Dublin. Whereupon, one of our learned friends leaned in and, no doubt with a certain sarcasm, offered that our friend, in stately repose, would cut a fine shape as a priest. Legend says that our man was heard to mutter: 'Oh no, at least a fucking Bishop.'"

We both turn as if to verify this with the Bishop, but it's hard to tell. He reclines, his forearms folded across his chest, a beatific smile on his lips, barely a slit of eyeball visible beneath those hooded lids. I take a last toke and flick the stub over the edge. "Heaven bound," I say, "Heaven bound." Way above us, a plane cuts through the sky, drawing a white line beneath nothing at all.

There's a neat segue. Recently I found myself in such a metal tube, shearing through the stratosphere, bound for more exotic locales. I was going to a seminar on the West Coast, if you must know, traveling solo, which is in the best company possible. Stretching my legs, strolling through the cabin, a set of features framed in red stubble jogged my memory. I couldn't believe it. It was Fitz. You'd swear we had been the best of pals to see us, all smiles and embraces, if the latter only gingerly. We turned to talking of the old days, without dwelling too long on those aspects that might remain painful. At last our time elapsed and a silence drew in. Fitz looked at me in that way of his, out of the corner of his eyes.

"I see you've still got the cowboy look, dropped the duffel coat, though."

"In truth, I think the coat was an early casualty. You never saw me mature."

"A sight to behold, I'm sure." He paused then, his head balanced on his bony fingers. His own sartorial elegance had greatly improved too, no longer the hairy armpatch jackets, the shiny trousers. I noticed a glint beneath the well tended cuffs of his shirt. A very expensive watch came into view. Oh, I'm not sure of the exact make, I sincerely never was 'into time', but it was very expensive.

Fitz's lips turned down and he wiggled the trinket, looked again at me, one eyebrow raised.

I made to move back to my own seat. "Nice watch," I said.

"Oh, this," said Fitz, examining it as though for the first time in ages, "I got this from my grandfather."

THE SECRET LOVER OF CAPT. RAYMONDO D'INZEO

All the songs that do be playing inside my head, from my father's gramophone or leaking out of the radio. On raucous nights on city streets, arm in arm in arm with Maisie and Trish, some young man might whistle in passing, or sing out from beyond the snug of a crowded bar. You'd hope that, once upon a time, the fella might sway out of the darkness and into the cone of light beyond, at the corner of the flats. Hands in his pockets, his hair and tie that little bit askew, singing just for you alone, something that only the two of you will know, something maybe in Italian.

Bells are chiming all over the Liberties. Smells are being cast by Guinness's Brewery. A burnished sky is pierced by the mitred spire of St Augustine's and John the Baptist, its twelve statues gazing impassively over all.

I know Robbie Egan is coming up behind me. I can hear his spokes whirring as I step into Frances Street and the cries of the hawkers die away with the last echoes of the bells. He circles me on his Findlater's bike, ogling and gurning. He's a clown, Robbie Egan, a beautiful, handsome clown.

"Hey Annie, will you be up at The Clock tonight?"

"I don't have the time," says I.

"Very good," says he, pulling out of his orbit. "You'll see me there when the small hand's at eight."

"And what'll the big hand be up to?"

He's cycling away now, waving one hand like a departing stage comic at the Theatre Royal, Tommy Dando playing him out. "That's for you to find out," he calls, weaving into the crowd.

He's no Prince Charming, but he sings to me sometimes. Booze ballads mostly, sometimes fancies himself with a Beat number. At heart, I'm an old fashioned girl. I like when there's a whiff of Sinatra off him. Hair slicked back with cabbage water, as Maisie would say, a boy lost in the Rat Pack. I'd rather a crooner though, or a handsome tenor. Robbie likes the Drinking Song from the Student Prince, mind; no surprise there really. Not that we're an item, not really. It's a game of cat and mouse, but who's the cat?

It was by Cassoni's, down towards Rialto, that he made his first move. I was walking out with Maisie, sharing a one-and-one, when he whistled from a lamppost. The smog fell like ammonia onto the street, streetlamps swelling like harvest moons strung from pole to pole.

"Go on," says I to Maisie. She gives me that knowing look, like she's a woman of the world.

I don't go to him, or anything like that. He takes just a step forward, into that cone of light. My heart clenches, then ebbs a little. He is drunk, swaying in his spotlit circle.

"Annie," he says, "this one's for you." He raises his cigarette arm as if to pluck notes from the thickening air.

> *'Twas down on Thomas Street, that I first met with Annie,*
> *The sun it was setting and the evening grew dark.*
> *Over Kingsbridge and beyond in a jiffy,*
> *My arms were around her up there in the Park.*

What can I do but laugh. The clown. Some of his mates whoop off by the corner and Robbie spins his gesture into irritation. He turns back to me, takes a long drag and sends words out with the smoke.

"What do you say, Annie? What's the chance, eh?"

"Chance would be a fine thing," says I, stalking after Maisie.

My Da used to take us to the Horse Show. He was an army man, an army boy he was called, even with his hair sprouting grey and three kids in tow. He could get a pass to the RDS, taking me in over the turnstiles. There we'd be, walking amongst the quality. He knew that I loved the horses, always did. I'm telling you though, he'd lard up his stories to impress his little girl. Pointing up to the judge's box, he'd tell us stories of Captain so-and-so, General this-or-that, Colonel Ponsonby-orse. All the great and the good that he'd rubbed shoulders with, back in the day.

But of all the people who exalted that great occasion, whether in story or in truth, there were none so great as the magnificent Italians. Their swagger and style, their stealthy beauty, and their leader: Captain Raymondo D'Inzeo. The Italians were kings of the ring. The Captain and his brother, Piero, leading them in their dashing uniform of the Carabinieri, guiding their mounts into the ring as tigers into a hunt. What magnificent beasts they were, Irish bred but changed in their contact with the Italians into something exotic. The greys really caught my fancy. The Rock with his imperious canter, Rockette gorgeously dappled, with swirling tail and flashing heels.

Maisie and Trish have their movie stars of course, Brando and Sinatra, Elvis and his swinging hips. Me, I've got my

Captain, stern of countenance, stout of heart, a man who is gentle and strong. A man who is the epitome of silence. The girls are vastly amused. They ask me: Annie, what horse does he ride?

"Rockette," I tell them, with a flourish to convey ... I don't now what.

"I know what Rock-ette he'd like to ride. A Royal-ette, more likely." Maisie laughs at her insinuation. She can be very coarse at times.

"I don't know about a Royalette," I says, "but I wouldn't mind having Captain Raymondo D'Inzeo on my back."

Oh, our laughter can be heard all the way down to the Liffey.

On days the Liberties might be cloaked in fog, an island floating in a sea west of the city. Most times, the air would smell of hops and yeast from the Guinness brewery, mingling with malt from the distilleries. When the wind was right, or maybe wrong, the stewing smell of death would creep in from O'Keefe's the knackers on Cork Street. If the sky was blue surely that was a ruse. God in his heaven had been caught napping and some mischievous angel had allowed the sun peep through. More often the sky roiled with smoke and fumes, or the fall of evening wrapped the town in smog. The spires and towers loomed above – the modern might of the Hop Store, the ancient turret of Saint Audoen's, the smokestacks and windmill tower of the brewery. Soaring above them all, the fulcrum around which the city spun: the mitred tower of John's Lane Church.

"It's the Church of Saint Augustine and John the Baptist," my Da would say. I knew of John the Baptist, of course, the man who baptised Jesus, but the other one ... According to my Da he was a very holy man, but much bothered by temptation.

"He would often say to God: 'Lord make me chaste, but not yet.'"

"What was he running from?" I asked.

"The English," he said.

He claimed that the spire was the highest in Dublin. God's own skyscraper it was, with the statues of the twelve apostles set in niches all the way to the top. My Da told me it was Patrick Pearse himself fashioned the statues and put them there. He had set emeralds in the eyes of the saints, the better to see the foreign foe approach. From that height they could see most of the ways to England, so they could warn if the lousers, as my Da said, tried to sneak up on us again. I knew from my history that they did. They must have come at night, I suppose.

Dad got me the job at Cassoni's in Rialto. That was years back and I was just a skivvy to begin with. Now I serves at the counter and in the sit-down cafe Mister Cassoni opened last year. My Da prepped me good at the time, giving me the history so as I wouldn't look like a daw.

"Remember," said he, "Mister Marconi, Guglielmo, came over at the turn of the century." He was the first man to bring the wireless to Ireland, according to Dad, who knew him, of course.

"But oh," I'd say, "it's Cassoni, not ..."

Clip on the ear. "Whisht! He had to change his name to go into hiding."

"But who was he hiding from?"

Pitying stare. The English, of course.

"They wanted the secret of the wireless, but Marconi was too clever. He went undercover right here, got a house in Reuben Street and smuggled the first set to Pearse in nineteen sixteen. The first wireless broadcast ever came from the GPO on the day of the Easter Rising. 'Irish men and Irish women!' aye, and Radio Eireann's still broadcasting from the same spot."

These details I never shared with Mister Cassoni, the great man's son. He had a surprisingly Italian accent, for someone reared in Reuben Street. His old man lived upstairs, you know, never said a word, just sat in an armchair all day, listening to music on the radio.

Many's the time and oft through Rialto I did stroll. I'd listen to the songs of bargees sweeping under Rialto bridge heading down to Portobello. The hawkers looking down from the banks, singing their response, like they were starring in a musical. Summertime, the boys would play wearing nothing but their Jockeys. They'd gather by the locks, plunging into the greasy water in turn. Animals they were, proud and white, the water jewelled on their bony hides. I'd see their faces looking up at me, like stoats stalking their prey. I'd hear their calls, feel all my follicles rise in anticipation. Oh lord, make me chased; and of course, I was.

Summer was waning and the Italians arrived. The big event of the week was the Aga Khan Cup. Teams of four horses and riders from four nations would compete for the prize. The Aga Khan himself would be there. The top brass would be in the judge's box. The Italians were determined to win it this year. As was their custom, they met in the days before at Cassoni's to plan their strategy.

The team would take the private room upstairs. This night, I remember, I was to serve them. The best of Italian food, specially prepared by Mrs Cassoni herself, everything exactly to their liking. The Italians in their homeland were less inclined towards fish and chips than you would think, especially the higher orders who considered such fare common. There would be assorted pasta plates, tagliatelli with pesto, spaghetti with Bolognese sauce, homebaked bread with garlic and herbs, parmesan cheese fine grated for sprinkling and thinly sliced Parma ham. Solely for these guests there would be a chilled bottle of white wine and another of red. The quality, unlike us, like to eat and drink at the same time.

They took little notice of me to begin with as myself and Mrs Cassoni brought in the trays. The Captain was presiding, resplendent in his uniform, his brilliantined hair smooth as paint on his noble head. He was at the head of the table, his brother, Pierro to his right, a less stern likeness of the Captain. To the left sat Graciano Mancinelli, fashionably dressed in the style peculiar to Italians, as we know from the Movies. At the far end of the table, in a sphere all her own, La Contessa Vittoria Rossi was arranged as certainly as a statue of Rome's golden age. She made me shake almost as much as the Captain. So beautiful and elegant she was, her hair set tight to her head sprouting dark ringlets at the flare of her neck. Out of her perfect face shone the icy gaze of deep blue eyes. Poised there, her cigarette held aloft on its tapered, onyx holder, a smile playing the corner of her lips.

Later, the room draped itself in smoke, formalities giving way to companionship. I served espresso as the Captain posed by the easel and clip chart, his Carabinieri jacket hanging from the stand. I could not help noticing the revolver and holster strapped to his ribs.

He smiled at me, patted his weapon. "You cannot be too careful," he said.

"Is it loaded?" I asked, though Mrs Cassoni had told me not to speak.

I heard Graciano laugh. The Captain looked at him sternly, then, softer, at me. He raised his hand, held it open against my chin.

"You cannot be Italian, with that freshness to your face, that russet tint to your hair. You must be Irish, which is perfectly fine. Bellissimo! Our blood mingles, has done for centuries, the Latin and the Celt. As you know, each of us around this table has an Irish mount, mine, the Irish filly Rockette. I have a taste for such fillies, Celtic of blood, wild of spirit."

That is what he said to me as the room spun around. Cross my heart and hope to die, which I very nearly did, right there. Then something passed between us and my blood blossomed as if bidden by summer. The Captain's hold ebbed into a gesture towards the door. I turned in silence and hurried out. As I passed I saw La Contessa fix me with her coldest glare.

I knocked off soon after. The team would leave discreetly when they chose. Mrs C could instruct the skivvy in the tidying up.

As I left, a drizzle fell from the swollen night sky. A figure whistled from the cone of a streetlamp, flicking his butt towards the gutter. With one arm he swung about the post in a half circle before launching himself at me.

"I'm singing in the rain," he sang, tapping his folded umbrella on the shiny pavement.

I sidestepped to walk by.

"Just singing in the rain." He attempted hooking his brolly on the bus-stop, missed, then disguised his stumble by tap-dancing onto the road.

I continued walking.

"What a glo-rious feel-ing," now a paradiddle of steps came tapping behind me, "I'm hap - happy again!"

"For God's sake, Robbie, use the umbrella as God intended."

With a confident flourish, he did so.

"Are you drunk?" I asked.

"Not yet," he pointed ahead. A pub glimmered at the corner of Rehoboth Place.

"It's late," I said.

"You never came the other night, to the Clock."

"I told you, I didn't have the time."

"Maybe your clock needs some winding," said he, cheeky as you like.

We are standing in shallow puddles on the terrazzo floor of Byrne's Select Bar. The barman in waistcoat and striped shirt polishes the copper counter to a painful gloss. I sit in the snug and Robbie carries the stout bottles through from the bar.

"What brings you to the Barn?" I ask.

"What do you think?" says he, sidling up to me.

"Mar dhea!" says I, all sarcastic.

"No, go on."

"Let's see," says I, "you thought you'd return the Findlater's bike late."

"Oh, I won't be doing that much longer."

"You're a bigger eejit than I thought, so."

"Ah now, Annie. Bigger and better things. I've landed a job with Bailey Gibson printers, up the Circular there towards Player Wills. Store job, driving a fork-lift. But here's the thing, if I get my driving licence, I could be out on the road. They do deliveries all over the county, good money." He rubs his fingers together, as though I can't grasp the concept.

For a change, I'm lost for words. Imagine, big, booby Bob getting himself a real job. He looks at me, reading my mind; I know, because his lips are moving. Ha! I'm joking. Seems he's not such a fool after all.

He smiles his best smile. Still a bit foolish, just the same, with all the beer inside of him. Raises his bottle and clinks it to mine. "Bottoms up, then. If you know what I mean."

So we are walking out, Robbie and me. There are prospects, all right. Robbie is a man with prospects. That Sunday morning, I meet him in Frances Street and we walk all the way past Pimlico and on to the Barn. We'll be going to the matinee at the Rialto, and after that, well, you know yourself.

> *Over Kingsbridge and beyond in a jiffy,*
> *His arms all around me up there in the park.*

Just past Cassoni's I see the car. It is an Italian sports, a red Alfa Romeo with the roof rolled down. Graciano is at the wheel, la Contessa Rossi languishing in the passenger seat, her hair blowing free. She signals the car to halt when she sees us.

"You," she calls. We had stopped by the cinema and I had turned my back on the road to read the coming at-tractions.

I hear a car door close. As I turn I know I will see her approaching. She stands before us, her cigarette poised.

She asks for a light. Robbie obliges, though she stays looking at me all the time.

"You," she says, "you have set your sight on the Captain. You are good. A young girl with well turned calf. But would he set his cap for you, the Captain? In all probability. He can acquire what he likes."

I can't think what to say. "Will Italy win the Aga Khan?" I stammer.

La Contessa puts her head to one side, like a bird looking at a worm. When she speaks, it is not by way of a reply. "I see your man there. He is within your reach. Don't take me wrong for, believe me, we both have love in our hearts. And yes, we will win."

"Vittoria!" Graciano calls from the car.

She turns, says something in Italian, and then looks at me again. She says nothing, just looks at me with meaningful intensity. Finally, she turns on her heel and climbs back into the car.

Robbie is at my shoulder. "What was that about?" he asks.

I link my arm in his. "Girl talk," I say.

La Contessa, from the passenger seat, has seen this gesture and she tilts her head back a little, just so. Then, in a flash of chrome and glass, bobbed hair and blue eyes, she is swept away. The car hums its throaty song, fading away from the bend by the Barn, disappearing off up towards Walkinstown, and the green hills beyond.

So, I ask you: What's a girl to do? Would I marry Robbie? Hitch my wagon to his dizzy prospects?

He has a good heart, does my Robbie. And he scrubs up well, cuts enough of a dash to turn many's the girl's head, but not too much, mind. It's his head will be turned when I walk up the aisle in John's Lane Church, my father beside me, sombre as a stick. It's Robbie that'll guide me out. We'll run to his Morris Minor with confetti raining down on us, drive off in the clatter of cans and the calls of friends.

We'll have a week away in a hotel by the strand. People will call us Mister and Missus. We'll be so old and so in love. Then our lives will start. They're building houses up in Greenhills, even as far away as Tallaght. And when we're settled, and when the money allows, he'll take me to a show at the Theatre Royal, or to a movie at the Metropole, sometimes even the Rialto, just like old times.

Of course, come autumn and there's only one place to go. We'll get tickets for the Horse Show in Ballsbridge, dress up in our finest and stroll amongst the quality. We'll get a ringside seat in the middle of the stand on the day of the Aga Khan Cup. Come the last round and the time bell rings. Stepping out from the paddock, we see the familiar figure in his Carabinieri uniform, riding the gingerish grey, Rockette. Then the hush and the hooves, brief silences marking the leaps through the air. We'll gasp as one when a pole is clipped, or when Rockette kicks back her heels, as she does. We'll rise together as they go clear, as the Captain stands on his stirrups, raising his cap to the judge's box.

His portrait is framed against the blurred background of a thousand faces. They may be lords and ladies, stars of stage and screen, they may have come in their Jaguars and mink, but they are only splashes of colour that a careless artist might throw. But I know my Captain, and the one face he'll see. Our eyes will meet across the distance and I'll smile to myself and for him. In all that colour and noise, I'll know who I am. And I'll know that whatever I do, whatever will be, that I will remain the secret lover of Captain Raymondo D'Inzeo.

THE WHITE HAIRED BOY

Out here on the periphery, stone piled on stone, marking the edge where the teeming magnet of the city meets its lonesome green hinterland. I recall balancing on that imagined rope, arms spread wide, a statue of the Saviour, walking heel to toe in the manner of a poised young girl. Wind poured down out of the wide emptiness, each sharp needle bolting me to earth. I was approaching the age where I was sure I could fly, but things became much less certain after that.

Birch trees had been planted along the red brick wall of the school. Their white skeletons glowed purple in winter, caught random shafts of sunlight in summer. The pathway was always dappled, shadows shifting in the air like the camouflage of an invisible beast. The girls' school was over there, redbrick ridged with green copper roofs, white spiked railings marking the territory. The church, massive factory of sturdy brick stood on a green hummock; the tower loomed to giddy heights holding its huge bell aloft. To the rear of our school, a castle stood guard, rising from a placid moat. Someone had left it there long ago. Still it lurked in some warp of space and time, looking out over the playing fields and factories to the motorway beyond.

Celt, Viking, Norman and English had fought in these fields, played their own games too, no doubt. New tribes followed. We came in our time, exuding that smell of freshness common to toys just ripped from their wrapping. I'd licked raindrops off those railings not long before, felt the first surge of sap rising on a spring morning. I'd donned the armour with the others in the changing-rooms beneath the Castle. I was ready to be a warrior, careless of myself.

***

I remembered the lane had been pure country last time I'd visited Cujo. I remembered that forgotten decade. Now, the city seeped into its stones. The fields that remained, even the odd surviving inhabited farm or cottage, were somehow infected, fading under the weight of an incipient illness. I had left the motorway but it remained within earshot, its constant hiss like a terrible river as I took the hairpin into the final rise. The road cut beneath stern pylons, coming at last to the still faintly picturesque hollow.

Cujo, true to form, sat in the porch – there was always something of the trailer-trash about him. Not that I mind. Hooch and cigarettes are fine by me. I barked and he smiled. "Ah, slummin' it, I see," he said, and asked me in.

The usual rituals were observed. The inevitable formalities following on from the event, the lachrymose meeting and parting of two dark-suited men on an avenue of Cypress trees. Talk turned to Wigsy, as it inevitably had to. What was he doing there? What was he thinking? What, for that matter, might we have done to avert it all? Ah, such questions, as if we two men, on the threshold of middle age, could refashion existence from a jumble of wishes.

"I don't know," Cujo said. "I guess he was just out on the headland, the wind blowing poetry out of his head."

That was a nice way of putting it. "Wigsy out on the headland. Makes me laugh."

Cujo looked at me from the corner of his eye. "It's a long swim from Howth to Bray. A long dive from that cliff as well."

I agreed that it was.

"His head was turned," he said with more consideration. "All those words, the bloody adulation. You should never let anyone inside your head."

I almost laughed. "Thought you might say something like that."

"Fucking spare."

I wasn't sure who he meant, exactly. He skinned up a rolly. More lined than unlined, I'd say. He bade me the honour of the spark. I declined. It was a long drive back.

"So, where to now," he wondered. "And then there were two. Aye?"

Where to now? The only place left to travel is time. We've been speeding along that landscape from the get-go, careless of reaching our destination. Except now there's a wall across the highway. I've been noticing that wall for some time. I know what it means. For an old goof like me, and Cujo there, the mad dog himself, there's only one way to travel that line; the way back.

***

What is it really? The past? A corridor lined with bullies and brassers, where men in black might loom with proprietorial malice, where doors might open to the flicker of lights and fleshy silhouettes, or something altogether more cold and dark.

Time was when we were three. Time was we were formed from the primordial soup, opposites attracting repulsively. There they were, Wigsy and Cujo, bold boys filling the corridor with shapes. I should have been their victim, blond and willowy, expectant. Wigsy gauging my weight, Cujo smiling, anticipating mirth. Yet, we fell in together, the three of us against the world, and Brother Eustace. He had our number early on, gathering the three of us up in his eyes at first sight. "Boys, oh boys, and who have we here?"

Wigsy was Peter Wigglesworth; just imagine the flak he got for that. Cujo was Joe Cooney, the Mad Dog. Me, I was Sean Cash, Johnny to my friends. Brother Eustace made great fun out of that. He'd look into me with his Arctic blue eyes, grasp my upper arm and lean in close enough to smear me with his liquorice breath. "But, would you put yourself on the line, boy? Would ye walk the line for me?"

There was always a relationship there, alright. You could call it charisma, I suppose, but with Brother Eustace I think it was something more primal. Useless? Yeah, he knew that one, bequeathed us the same epithet straight to our faces, relishing the irony. There was love there too, though you didn't want to blink and miss it. You could call it love; after all we were the class who, for the first time ever, got to the final of the County Cup.

The County Cup was the Holy Grail. The one craved-for laurel, sporting or academic, that had eluded the old school. Of all the men in black, or parents, alumni or undergrads, Brother Eustace was most keyed up for it, more than was natural. He wasn't even from the County. Nor, strictly speaking, was it the formative sport of the school. Still, the thing had developed a cachet; it became for our own backwoods the Sam Maguire, the Jules Rimet, the Stanley Cup. Our name had never been etched on it, and we'd had good teams in the past. It floated out of reach, unobtainable, the receptacle of our dreams and ambitions.

Then came our team, *the* team. And I was the white-haired boy. Would I die for Brother Eustace? Hey, I was in the prime of my warrior years. Death was my duty, my joyous anticipation. Ra, ra, roo, be true to your school. Ra, ra, ree, be true to your team!

As each challenge on the rickety ladder to the final loomed, Brother Useless would give the team talk. Calling on the saints above to lend us guidance, the devils below to give us fear. Most of all, he painted on that vast canvas of unexperienced dreams, carved our futures, indelibly.

"Oh, ye'll be indelible, boys. Ye will be the indestructible heroes of your Alma Mater. Immortal as those men on your picture cards. Consider this, boys, consider this when you pass down that corridor, that hallowed corridor hung with those heroes of field and track, scholarship and science. Ye know them well, the white-haired boys who look out each year from the glass. To them ye are but ghosts, and they to ye are gods. Join them boys, be the handsome faces to press on glass, to stare down ghosts and chimera forever and a day."

Oh, we were in thrall, all right. All our disaffection from the ruling clergy evaporated. We were the anointed, the elite, the very elect; pouring down the tunnel like pure fire, to the cool, green icing of the field of dreams beyond.

Oh, I'm telling you, some of the poor cunts would be pitching tents.

***

"What became of you, then?" Cujo asked.

I looked at him, lounging there, smiling through the beers. "Sláinte," I said, tipping cans. "You know yourself, the fuckers."

"Fuckers plural?" Cujo looked at me, evenly.

Who'll I put it down to, then? To my old pal, Wigsy, the little rat? Then there's Brother Eustace, the king rat.

There's a story I do tell, far more fascinating than the sordid details of the other thing. Telling of the time I snuck down to the park one night, one dark night in the aftermath.

Stealing past the palisade they've built to stop the green icing flowing into the Valley, where the river cuts a scar deep down in the shale, I fancy I see the moon skate uncertainly over its black swift waters. It's all pitch black out there, save the arena. Floodlights describe a cube of bristling green and glare, a jewel in the night. Then I see him, the new white-haired boy.

Long after they'd all gone: team, kit-men, balls and all, our friend remains. Do you know what he was doing? Eh? I'll tell you. When the floodlights go out, there's just a cone of light from the lamp standard by the clubhouse. It's enough to put some shape on the penalty area. There he is, standing on the spot. Practicing.

That's good, It's normal, up to a point. Listen. At the corner of the goal he sets a candle, a foot in from the post. The candle's lit.

Not much light from that, I hear you say.

108

Listen. He takes the penalty, right. Time after time, the same thing.

Aiming at the candle?

Not quite. Just above it, but close enough to snuff out the light. Pufff... In the shadow of the Castle, deep into evening as the colour leeches from the field of dreams, under Brother Eustace's gimlet glare, the most trusted of acolytes makes the final preparations.

"Did he really do that?" Cujo wanted to know. "All that mumbo-jumbo?"

What a boy wouldn't do, to be the white-haired boy.

It was different in the days when I was the white-haired boy. Those were the days in the dungeon, the sweat and the studs, the stink and camaraderie. I wallowed in the mud, stayed clean within. Now I was all inside out.

Smoking in the shed, spitting at the crows. Everyone knows the incident, a bottle of smoke. Well, they thought they knew. There was a bottle, at least, and there certainly was smoke. Was there fire, though? Was there fire? Why bother returning there with all its crummy sentiment? Why should I be a smooth statuette, gold plated and sexless? I'm telling you, I'd hairs in places you wouldn't believe.

***

The pub nestled by the old canal and was named for the lock nearby. I see colourful barges there, paint peeling under an idle sun. A pony-tailed man pulls on a rolly, flexes his tattoos and smiles our way. Or maybe his old lady glances up from tending her plants, or the hound barks. I can close my eyes and it returns to now: blocks of flats growing out of the ragworth, metal men raising arms to the sky. It was countryside then, pure country for sure.

A lane led down from the grounds where the County Final would play out, past farmhouses, junkyards and onto the canal. Cujo and I marked the trees, plotted our escape. The auguries were good. Us senior boys were free to explore, to mooch, sneak out back of the stand for a fag if the mood took us. Only the juniors were corralled, under the beady eyes of the men in black. Brother Eustace perched on the touchline, angel of death. Oh, my mind wandered to the field, out there where I'd left my dreams. "Ye-hay Wiggs-ay!" I roared. But his eyes gazed out to the horizon. Our Boys took to chanting. A scuffling jazz beat for the boggers mooching past, a chorus of barks when some of their girlfriends teetered by. Cujo had a hand on my elbow. It was time.

The bar was empty when we got there. A static-soaked screen sparked high in the corner, dust motes twirled downward in shafts of sunlight. The barman polished glasses, as if it mattered. Orders and glasses passed with few words, Cujo going for the pint, me for a shandy. "Right," said Cujo, "be a daredevil." The mood lightened and the drinks were set down.

"Lads, there's a quieter room at the back."

"Quieter than here?" Cujo adopted an awed tone. Somewhere, beyond the eerie sound vacuum, traffic hummed, a distant crowd throbbed.

The publican cleared his throat. "The back, lads." There was a note of pleading, or finality. "I'll send in Joanne with the Dansette."

The room was down a dog-leg corridor, dropped three steps down to an older interior. Through the heavy door, it had the look of a forgotten residents' lounge. The girl came in with the portable record player. Joanne, or Jo-Anne, perhaps his daughter. Pleasantly curved, haphazardly coiffured, she was, like us, paused on that precipice between yearning and knowing. There was something else there, beneath that soft, blushing surface. A singularity in a white blouse, a dark star.

She didn't seem to like me much, casting surreptitious looks at Cujo, half smiling when I was only half watching. Man, I was pitching a tent, though. Just looking at her, aesthetically like.

Cujo, it seemed, grew bored. Implied excessive disdain for something she spun on the turntable. It was Fleetwood Mac, their Albatross, with its hypnotic beach-bum bass. He gathered up his tobacco pouch, made a show of sauntering out to the yard.

Some unseen wave had swept her closer to me. Two of us together on the upholstered couch. It was remarkable how hot the atmosphere can get with just breath and a thumping bass. That, and her hand rubbing my thigh, the fact that I was tracing the outline of her bra through the fabric of her blouse.

"Take it off, she said.

I worked on the top button.

"No," she accomplished that with less fuss. "No, take those off."

I glanced towards the door. She shrugged, figured he should be gone a while. She laughed. I stood and dropped them. What the hell; if you've got it, flaunt it. She bent towards it, something terribly interesting there. I wondered. What was it that so attracted in the hard parting of her hair? Drawn back severely into the sign of the cross.

"Oh God, oh my God," I cried, unsure if there was anyone there, unsure if I wanted there to be. That was when all heaven broke loose.

When at last I emerged back into the daylight, Cujo threw a baleful eye at me from his perch on a keg in the yard out back. Taking one last drag of his cigarette he flicked it expertly into the shore.

"What's the story?" I asked.

"I thought I heard some shouting and roaring. Figured someone had scored."

I looked away. "Whatever."

"Mind you, it wasn't as ecstatic as all that."

There he was, milking it for all its worth. I checked the angle of the shadows in the yard, sniffed the ozone in the air. "Must be near time now," I said. Something else though, I had heard that same strangled roar, as the door swung to. "Nobody's scored," I said. "Not yet."

We both looked off to the West. Out there, past the carpark, along the road by the dancehall to where the town faded into nothingness, the field of dreams waited. A deathly hush had descended, pulling low clouds in over the remnant of the day.

***

A boy remains. Arms outstretched he teeters on the thin white line, the net a web behind him. Out there on the periphery, he is the focus of all our pity and fear, a statue on the thin white line of the periphery. Cinder block on cinder block, the wall rises up from the marches. The sentinel is unmoved, his ice blue eyes level with the horizon. It is time for the white-haired boy to step forward into that circle of light, into the focus of destiny.

There is a thud, ominous or propitious, who can say. The sphere rises and rotates, shakes from its surface a myriad of droplets. It rises from the green lawn into the emptiness above. The breaching roar is caught in a cusp. A universal gasp falls toward that expectant hush. In silence, sharp as tinnitus, you sense that everyone must drop to their knees, hands clasped to ears, eyelids pressed shut. But, that cannot be. No, all time becomes one, all faces are open, mouths open, eyes wide.

The heavens leak rain and sunlight in equal measure. The air is physical, liquid amber, ready to fossilise all it contains. Each droplet retains a perfect copy of existence, each copy pregnant with a different possibility. Within each is the same sphere, poised, throbbing, an umber heart shaking loose its satellites of blood and tears.

THE BLACK MOON

It was a postcard, though not quite so straightforward on closer viewing. Not strictly commercial. More arthouse and internal. The picture was in black and white, but mostly black. It reminded me of a still from some old movie, in a way; though the subjects and setting were present day so far as I could tell. There was a window, a bay window, leaking light into a room. Beyond that, what could have been a harbour, bleached in the sun.

So far, so banal. What struck about the image, though, was the couple arrayed inside the window. A young man and a young woman both reclining, facing each other with the pure empathy of lovers. It could be a painting in its stillness, in the certainty of its composition. Yet, there is nothing self conscious about the arrangement. They are two contemporary people lounging in a bay window, nothing more.

What was it to me, anyway? I had moved into the new house and spent the morning rounding up those forgotten things. Things the previous owner might have dumped, but hadn't bothered. Vacant possession after all, means vacant possession. The card was in a biscuit box left inside the hot press. There were others with it, of course. You would think I should forward them to the previous owner, but I'm not sure that's an option.

I flicked over the card to look for a clue. This hardly eased the cryptic quality of the thing. Florid writing in a florid hand. Still, captivating in its own sweet way.

That old love song. We'll meet over a bottle of wine. You'll see it all so clearly. X –

It was unsigned, no dear or darling, only this address, my new address: Four Winds, Vico Road, Killiney, County Dublin. Even the stamp had been lifted so that I could not tell the postcard's age. I turned it over again. No, didn't get it. There was a secret here for sure, some history between sender and recipient. But it was destined to stay hidden.

Curious though, why anyone would send such a message in plain view through the post. But hey, why should I care? It was a fragment of an unknown life and so unimportant as to be discarded by the last occupant. I was the new occupant, happy to spend the morning replacing the old dusty junk of the attic with junk of my own.

The things we can never throw away: concert tickets and travel stickers, car magazines and girlie magazines and music fanzines, letters never sent and letters never answered, the black leather jacket called Boris and the gold lamé tie. Boxes, bags and bundles of jagged and rounded memories, clinging like limpets to the hull of some old schooner.

Who would believe it? From bedsit minstrel to man of property. An overnight sensation! I was made up, though some feigned disdain. Jessica had laughed when she heard. Called me Lord of the Manor, amongst other things;

although the house was hardly so grand for me to merit such entitlement. She could await her invitation, the bitch.

I know, I know, a bit harsh. We've had our moments, Jessica and I. Had our bit of fun. There was that joke. I would introduce her as my first wife. Or, this is my current wife. Of course, we never married. That was an issue with the gossip columns. With the comics. No, never married, just explored.

So now I slouch in the bay window of the lounge and am soothed by the waves below. The kettle whistles in response to a passing gull, or is it that the gull ... I pour the water for an instant coffee. Jessica would have demanded filtered, made an elaborate ritual from it - but I am too impatient for that. She would also have seen to it that I had an ashtray and not slopped my ash into the half full matchbox on my lap. Jessica would have crowded.

I began to sift through the bundle of old postcards I had yet to throw out. Snapshots of well known places from unknown people. The previous owner – now there was a strange fish, a funny onion. Had she left in a hurry or simply forgotten her treasure? Or just not bothered? There really wasn't all that much up there: clothes and scarves, an old radio, an empty bell jar and other bric-a-brac, some books I might read. So, why did she leave? The estate agent had flexed his jaw as though that was not a question asked in polite company. Who knows? Restless? These artistic types, you know yourself. He had the grace to offer me an apologetic blink.

She must have been a magpie, a collector, as very few of the cards were addressed to Four Winds and practically none, it seemed, intended for the same person. To John, to

Maisie and Bob, The McCormacks, Carlo and gang, all at 73 - and so on. But were there any by name to her?

Unless – Fifi, having a wonderful time – and a composite picture of Athens. And that could be the same Fiona, informed that the Piazza San Marco is a carousel but all the canals stink. That was her and that was here. Fiona is the better of the two. Fifi is slightly fake, toydogs in handbags, that type. But Fiona might walk her pet panther after dark.

Jessica, meanwhile, is almost too beautiful to touch, a pearl, a solo moon that waxes and wanes. Touch her I do, if never often enough, playing chords on her highly strung nerves; my muse, who never phones nor writes - but waits. While Fiona, if that is her name, does not exist. She cannot be held or manipulated or understood. She shines no light on me. She carries no torch. She is the darkness I am reaching for.

I am back with the sounds of the sea below my home. The feeling of death recedes but I remain fascinated by the card and its message. I pin it to the cork board I have hung in the kitchen for such things. I hope it will go away.

It does not. It remains alone on the board to glare at me each time I enter the kitchen. Throughout the house I sense its presence, hear it whisper its message. Each time I sit in silence and solitude I find my visions inhabited by the image of that couple entwined, yet not quite entwined.

The image is the epitome of comfort. Where silence reigns and the spying artist is treated with cool indifference. What are you looking at, after all? You wish to be there, within that sensuous tableau, but cannot be part of it. Images are locked within those words on the reverse. Old love songs and their elusive refrains. Old liaisons rekindled over a bottle of wine. Candles in the moonlight and bodies become one in flesh. They haunt the songs that play on the radio.

After three weeks I break my self-imposed house exile and ring Jessica. She is not pleased to get my call. It is the telephone paradox; the more we wait and long for a person to call, the more venom we reserve for them when eventually they do.

With Jessica, her insecurity stretches tight like a drumskin over her emotions. The drum beats insistently if I let more than a week pass and fear stalks her of things that might have offended me, of others who may have siphoned me into their lives, of other lovers and sundry disasters that can befall a man in Jessica's life.

"I thought you were dead," she said.

I know that I must do something to allay her panic and so agree to meet, although that had not been my plan. She wants to call up but I veto that. We agree to meet in town. In Neary's just off Grafton Street.

I am outside. A cast-iron naked lady holds her torch aloft for me. Perhaps I am somewhere else. Veils of drizzle drift in over the street. A tramp importunes me, as is customary. Jesus Christ, is there no rest? I never give. Why throw good money after bad? I don't remonstrate, a shrug is all. What can I do?

He stops and stares. He'd be about my age, but he looks a hundred years old. Oh my God, don't tell me! I fumble quickly for my fare. A note. I'll give him a fiver. I'm a bigshot, after all. His eyes open wider. He knows me! I offer a piece of advice.

"Don't spend it all on booze and broads."

Those pale blue eyes. All the lines of his face point there. A smile is tugging at those lines, not necessarily the right type of smile.

"I'll take your money," he says, sneaking away. "But as for your advice ..." He has turned his face away and drifted down to the street corner. There, faded in the rain, he raises both arms and shouts at the sky: "You can shove your advice up your hole!"

I am impressed by the length he holds the last word. Almost operatic. I flick the cigar butt after him. Oh, I suppose he'll blow it all on booze, whatever about the broads. Who knows what they do down there. Who cares? Let him spend it on more drink. It's what I would do.

Shouldn't there be a lady with a lamp? Someone to watch over me. The night is too foggy. Even inside the bar, the fog sags from the ceiling, like back in the day when people smoked indoors. I walk in a muffled hubbub. There is drink taken, then more walking within interior and exterior fog. A soft moon appears above and slowly hardens into an antique lamp. The Lady! The lady must be holding it aloft. But there is only a disembodied arm holding up the lamp. I enter Neary's.

Jessica is never punctual and I am not surprised that there is no sign of her in the crowded pub. Yet I feel strangely desperate and push through veils of smoke looking for that gypsy face, those hurt and suspicious eyes. What if my muse suspects that I am having an affair with a woman who does not exist? It does not bear thinking about and I elbow my way to the bar and call a pint of Harp.

"Are you going to play it for us?" Paddy, the barman, asks.

"If it doesn't take you all night tuning it," I snap. Recognition is an occupational hazard and I align my stool to give the best view of the huge mirror behind the bar where I can see the door without being seen. There is a clang in the distance and Paddy catches my eye, motioning me to the phone.

The area by the callbox is heavily populated and I have to strain to hear.

"Where in all blue fuck were you?"

"I'm here. I was here."

"Liar."

"Ah now, Jess."

"I thought I'd drop up to see the place, see if you were here. But you had already left." The voice is so soft that I wonder if I am really hearing it, but it's Jessica alright.

"Jessica, where are you?"

"So I let myself in. You were always so careless with what you own, and what you leave lying around."

"Are you in my house?"

"It is beautiful here, but I won't stay. I got your letter, by the way. I'll leave a note, you like messages."

She had found it, the bitch, that card was becoming a curse. "Listen," I told her. "Stay where you are. I'm coming straight home."

"Bring a bottle," she said, and hung up.

There are things that a Jensen can do that make it more a weapon than a car. Weaving through the traffic I would easily have made it home within thirty minutes. My mind raced as the streetlights streaked past and the absurdity of my situation hit me. Hard to believe that a postcard should cause such chaos. But for that old love song and that scribbled note – I meshed the gears at an amber light and something lurched in the pit of my stomach. I had the curious feeling that I was evaporating.

A metal pedestrian bridge raced towards me. A familiar figure staggered, clanking along the walkway; a wino no older than myself. But he looked a hundred years old with his grizzled beard and wizened face.

From his coat he pulled a bottle of cheap red wine, a fiver from the Late Nite on Camden Street. From his mind he plucked a song that had been popular some years before, long before he had ever started out on the bridge. It was one of our songs, the soundtrack for those early days of love between Jessica and I. Most people know it and call it that old love song - but the wino sang it with all the irony it deserved, howled it to the black new moon he knew was up there somewhere.

Between verses he sucked at the bottle until the bottle chuckled at being sucked dry. Cursing, the wino swung, lashed out at the wind and the night and crashed, exhausted, against the parapet. The bottle squirmed from his fingers and teetered on the edge. "One... green...bottle," he moaned as it plummeted into the darkness below.

I saw the glass splinter across the road. If it had all shattered perhaps everything would have been okay, nothing but sharp frost on the motorway. But the heavier base was made of sterner stuff, and inserted itself standing jaggedly upright in my path. It was this that ripped the front right tyre open. Speed did the rest.

I am nothing now, just gas inside a fiery missile. I will be the ghost inside the machine. As the world spins a circle around me I look back and see the grizzled beard and wild staring eyes imprisoned by the railings on the bridge.

His lips twitch, as if still singing that old love song - perhaps he still is. These things go on forever. The words escape me. Yet, I look back and see it all, so clearly ...

A MAN WALKS INTO A BAR

A man walks into a bar. I should know. I'm working the tiny bar, a telephone booth at the bottom of a flight of steps. You can't help but see who comes in. Not many do, but it doesn't take many to fill the place. Sometimes I get talking to them. It's like that in confined spaces. Men mostly, sinking shots or bottled stout, women too, though rarely. Thing is, it's just a door off the street, then a flight of steps to a smoke pit at the bottom. I'd guess a woman prefers to see what's seeing her. If you catch my drift. There's that predator and prey thing. A woman'll come in and sit at the bar, with a cocktail or a glass of chilled white. Might look good sitting there in the gloom, though some of them, up close, would haunt the house for you. There'll be the odd peach in a parcel of prunes. Like I say, odd.

Anyway, this night it's quiet and there's not a soul. And a man walks into the bar. Goes up to the bar and orders a Manhattan. "Well," says I, "we do a good one here. Breakfast of Champions."

He sits right there. An ordinary man, five nine, five ten, mousey hair and a suit jacket over open-necked shirt and slacks. Late forties, I'd guess, or turned fifty; going to seed a little. So, I fix him the Manhattan and tell him the charge. He takes a swig and looks at the docket. I'm polishing some glasses and he's drumming his fingers on the counter. Here it comes, I think; same old, same old.

The man looks at me with those washed out, grey eyes of his and says.

"Did you hear the one about the polar bear walks into a bar?"

"There's only one?" I say.

"Polar bear walks into a bar, goes up to the counter and orders a Manhattan. Barman fixes him the drink and charges him. Polar bear takes a slug." Here, my man, jiggles his glass and raises an appreciative smirk. "And it's a damn fine Manhattan too, I'd say."

"The polar bear says?"

"No, the polar bear says nothing. Barman turns to the bear and says: Say, we don't get many polar bears in here. To which the bear replies: At the price of the fucking drink, I'm not surprised."

Well, I'd heard it before but laughed anyhow. I fix him another and we fall into talking. The night wears on. People come and go. As things turn out, I get to like the man. Or maybe I become mesmerised. We are alone by the end of the night as we were in the beginning. I turn off the television above the bar. The man had been watching it on and off as I worked the counter and what few customers there were. By way of apology, I joke about it being a conversation killer. He stubs out his cigarette and says, apropos nothing:

"You know that film? Robert Redford, I think. He's a big wheel in Vegas and he offers this guy, this tourist, a million bucks to sleep with the guy's wife."

"Yeah, whatshisname? Woody from Cheers."

"That's it; the husband, not the wife. Right, so where's the dilemma? It's a no-brainer. Shit, I'd sleep with Robert Redford for a million bucks."

I point out that movies are often like that. That sort of a scenario. The what if. Hey, we're talking it now. Money and love. Money and death and the whole damned thing.

"Okay. Here's a thing," he says. "Say someone was to say to you. A million bucks to kill a man. What'd you say?"

"Straight ethics there, bud. You're talking taking a life."

"Ah! And that would be a sin. A sin! Rickitty tickitty tin." He makes a mock paradiddle on the counter.

"Yes."

"But this man deserves to die. He's a bad man." He begins to laugh. "Does that not erode your ethic?"

"Who's to say he's a bad man?"

"The law."

"The law's an ass."

"Ha. You should know." He gestures to the now empty room.

I shrug. "Yeah, tell me about it." I think of the lawyers and Department spooks we get in here.

"Okay. The Almighty then. The man above says so."

"Well, Hallelujah! Praise the Lord."

"Oh ye of little faith," he shakes his head as though disappointed. But there's a light in those eyes.

I make closing up shapes. The smoke is thinning and the heat is waning. I turn the lights on full.

"Oh ye of little faith," he says again, rising from his stool. He leans on the counter, looking a bit drunker now, and older. He leans towards me. "The point is: for your heart's desire. All you have to do is kill a man, a very bad man, and he will give you your heart's desire. Sláinte".

His glass is empty but he pulls a slim silver flask from his jacket pocket and adds a dram. I raise an eyebrow. I am stern about such things. He motions for me to partake.

I demur. A thought occurs. Something that's been bothering me. He will give me my heart's desire? That's a different contract than before. He proffers a note. Again, I demur. He insists. "For yourself," he says.

I turn to put it in the till. The law and the Lord. Are they not all the one? I look up at the mirror behind the bar. Inscribed by a distillery, mottled with age and obscured by bottles, yet it offers me the panorama of the bar. It is empty of reflection. I have a dread that I will turn and see him still there. That was the thing that bothered me. The way that age and colour were capricious in his vicinity. The man who walked into the bar but did not walk out of the bar. The man who vanished.

Only his flask stood there. I picked it up, turned it over. Engraved on it, faint with use, were two words: Drink me. I smiled. How absurd. The faint odour of ... Brandy? I took a sip. My heart's desire. To think, a stranger was going to give me my heart's desire.

There was this woman who walked into the bar and ordered a Blue Lagoon. She would sip it and smoke. She had that way of smoking, her face angled down, as if reading a book. She'd exhale furiously. Times you'd think a steam train had pulled in.

She was certainly a looker. There was a past there too, though. Times she looked at you and you could see yourself having sex with her. Two silhouettes in a penthouse suite, beneath the neon sign on the roof that flashed on and off. Then the blinds would come down, the mercury would drop.

Of course we fell into that long distance conversation that's the lingua franca of bars across the meridians of time and distance. The usual? Set 'em up, Joe. A penny for your thoughts. You catch my drift?

A horse walks into a bar. Sits up at the counter and looks off into space. The barman asks: Why the long face?

She'd smile, and tell a little story of her own. One thing led to another and there we'd be, silhouettes making love in the penthouse suite, beneath the neon sign flashing on and off above the city.

The mercury drops as I climb the stairs at the end of the day. I emerge into snow. The streets are grasped in hush. The stars slip from their moorings and fall earthwards. I imagine my heart's desire in this landscape: a spooky moll, all Russian hats and ermine rolls, pistols in her suspenders and poisoned stilettos. All the fun to be had inside my head.

In truth, I remember she did something shady in the Department nearby: that Stalinist pile ennobled with its sculpted reliefs of heroic labourers and inexorable machinery. I guessed she seduced exotic marks in her own sweet way. Laying back on silken sheets she'd think of Hibernia, seduce them till they were unconscious and the microfilm inappropriately concealed.

I see her standing in the pulsing window, looking sadly at the money proffered on the bedside table. She looks over her shoulder so's all you'll see are the heavily shaded eyes.

"It is too much," she whispers. "But you forget. All ze money in ze vorld, vill not take ze place of love."

She doesn't speak like that, of course. I just made that up. It's colour. Christ, they don't call this Hibernia for nothing. My throat ignites with the coldness of it all. Again, I catch her looking at me under those heavy lids. A smile plays her lips. "Vot must it be like, to be running inside your head?"

There it is. The Russian accent again. She wasn't even Russian. She was from Dun Laoghaire, I think, and they're never in much of a hurry out there. I laugh and nearly choke on the frozen air. It's so cold, lawyers have their hands in their own pockets. I gain the door of my apartment block. All is quiet. Hush, hush. I draw carefully on the air and let my soul subside in the urban gloom, the flat, yellowed monochrome of the deserted city, all shadows banished by the neon and snow. But shadows await in the gutters and the doorways, waiting to fall from the sky beyond the parapet. I take the flask from my pocket, look it over again. Hey, that idiot won't mind. I take another slug. But there's something wrong. I had thought the fire in my throat was due to the cold. No, it wasn't that. How could I be so dumb? It's not like I'm the sort of man who wants for a tipple. Dammit, I'm a sucker for charming strangers.

I scramble up the stairwell, too panicked to wait for the lift. By the time I reach my door, I am starting to retch. Somehow, I negotiate the lock, and fall into the welcoming hardness of the tiled bathroom. My entire body struggles to escape its cage. There's not a thing I can do to stop it.

The voice comes from afar. At first, no more than the wind moaning, and then the wind delivering scattered monologues from street or stairwell, from flickering televisions behind the checkerboard windows of apartment blocks across the city at night. The voice grows closer. The voice is inside my head.

"How do you think it feels, to be stuck inside your head?"

I cannot reply. You would think I would know that one.

"Stuck inside one small orb, in a sticky web of synapses. How do you think it feels to be a marionette? Condemned to perform sexual feats upon your avatar, voracious and athletic beyond the scope of reason. Feats I would never consider within the hours of meat and machines. Those hours and days, those years of insomnia, within that cranium, without enough room to swing a cat. How do you think I feel about that?"

Listen to the false silence of the night; the masking static searching for life, for radios to invade, cicadas to rouse from slumber. That silence lengthens to an extended ping, becomes the swelling beep of tinnitus, then fades to black. How do I feel about that?

See me lying naked and prone, slick with that envelope of mucous. I hear you say: "Oh, it's you. It's you! It was always you." At least, I'm sure that is what I hear you say. Then again, while I shivered naked in a coating of slime, it's possible the words were diced and rearranged in a more meaningful way.

After some time, the roaring of the air quells and a silent yellow light soaks in. I get up and shower, let all the waters flow and drain the filth off my body. I touch myself there, but without the same pleasure as before. What is before? Everything is new, but obviously used. I lean against the full-length mirror. It is well steamed, so perhaps it's just the soft focus, but surely something is missing. Something altered. I look directly at my own gaze. I know these eyes.

Galaxies explode out there beyond the horizon, the punctuation points of a long but definable sentence. Time is the true infinity. Our allotment is the snake devouring itself, top to tail within a lifetime. Only at birth and death are we complete, at one with the infinity of time, and ready to begin the meal all over again

There was no sign of you when I emerged. Typical of the man in the morning. Nothing left for me but to return to the humdrum. I fuss with my clothes. All those straps and hooks, the tautness of elastic, the yielding ephemera of satin and lace. If I were a peacock I'd preen. I draw a new face and melt into the mirror.

I take a stroll through Stephen's Green of a morning. Stop at the Pagoda to smoke a menthol cigarette, watch the Chinamen unload their cargo. Later, I'll lounge amongst them in Belle Epoque bars and opium dens. All polished pewter and tiffany lamps, underlit tables throwing light up onto smiling faces. Mucha did the stained glass here, sinuous sylphs growing from metal plants, clothing permanently awry, yet chic.

Afterwards, as the city begins to empty, I repair to The Chopstick. The Chinaman that runs it is somehow distinctive. It's in his look; the sly eye, the discreet smile, his oily dynamism. He has that way of standing over you as you eat; proprietorial, deferential.

I order the Special Chow Mein. When it arrives I let the steam bathe my face, then I examine the entrails and curlicues for some stab of recognition. The Chinaman has materialised at my shoulder. I ask him what is in the Special. Some unfortunate equine corpse drowned in mustard is my guess.

"Pork," he says.

"Yes, but ..." I make a circular motion with my fork. There is much more besides, surely.

"Pork," he says again. "Pork! Pork! More pork!"

I hear laughter from the kitchen.

We become confederates, the Chinaman and I. It is something symbiotic. A shared sense of being outside, a sympathy for the need to subvert, the identity and repulsion of the other. I do whatever it is I do. Our conversation is limited.

To begin with, concerning the name of the premises – why just one chopstick ? You may well ask. Don't you need two? But perhaps the Chinaman never had both chopsticks in the chow mein. If you catch my drift. Having endured his running commentary on my meal, it is my turn. I sip my Blue Lagoon. "A man walks into a bar," I tell him and he cocks an eyebrow. "He says ouch, it was an iron bar."

"Ah, very good." He wags a finger at me. "Very good. I see. A man walks into a bar. Ha Ha."

"No, it's the next line," I say.

"A man walks into a bar. Ha ha. It's so funny."

"No, it's the next line." I insist.

Then a frown. "Stupid woman," he mutters, lifts my glass and leaves. He'll be back. I have use for him.

The thing is, that the thing is missing. Folded away to nothingness. I don't seem to miss it all that much. Which is weird. I still get the urge, but can always get a penis to go there. Man, that's so easy. Still, what's a girl to do? I must maintain some standards.

I am the girl who walks into the bar. But which bar? I examine the neon forest searching for the auspicious sign. Yes, lovers entwined, the king of my heart's desire. I find him at last, drinking rum from a bottle in a dockland casino. Do they make them like this any more? One-eyed men holding on for dear life to barrels, old stogies littering the floor. Darts thump the bristle somewhere out the back, and ribald cheers greet the kissing of men in shorts on a flickering screen.

So, there he is as he always was, in some scrote of a casino playing the machine. I know he sees me as I circle. I know this amuses him greatly. He indicates the stool at his side when at last I drop the pretence of searching.

"That reminds me," he says, in a WC Fields type of drawl. "A penguin goes into a bar." Here, he swivels to the floor, waddles on the spot in a way that's almost endearing. "And the penguin walks up and down the length of the bar, turning his head this way and that." He resumes his seat, mops his brow. "So the barman comes over and says, to the penguin: Hey, what's the problem here? And the penguin says, I'm looking for my brother. At which the barman, all eaten up with concern, says. What's he look like?"

It's then I know I'll have to kill him.

I've been separated too long from the herd. The zebras spook and keep their distance. Predators snooze in the long grass, flashing their teeth in juicy yawns. There are liaisons. A secret whiskey in a sun burnished snug, knees touching accidentally on a train. I am conscious of how new all this is, but still soiled. The damage love and loss has left. The desperation of that perpetual pursuit. I find myself on my knees in some alley on a Saturday night. On my back in a strange room as the sun comes up. All wrapped up and freezing on the Bull Wall, the wind at my back as I clatter home on slick cobblestones.

I strip naked before I kiss the mirror goodnight. I write with my lipstick on the mirror, so's I'll remember in the morning. It was you. It was you. Always you. Maybe it's because I miss you. You're a pebble, still rolling around inside my head.

But there is only one route back to my heart's desire. The streets are full of lupine men in reefer jackets, with nascent beards and uncombed hair, but I have found my mark and I know what to do. I dress to kill. I take to wearing lingerie, possess an instinctive aplomb in rolling on stockings, fastening garters fore and aft, bustier that pinches here and pushes up there. I raise my arms and perform the quick and delicate task of balancing the folds of my hair within the jewelled prongs of a lethal comb. I am everything you ever desired and more. Watch me now as I snare a bigger catch.

My peripheral vision is alive with flaming visions. I see him climbing from the car, eyes searching heavenwards to that rectangle of light where I should be. But what does he see through those slats? Some awful neon tableau, the small screen flickering in its cathode pulse, a lava lamp in full flow, a dying spider plant against a backdrop of peeling flock paper.

I dim the lights and let my claws scuttle across his well filled suit. When he leans closer I whisper Russian poetry in his ear. I let him fooster with the clasps as long as I can bear, then allow my clothes to fall in a pool around my feet. I gesture to the bed and he sits on it and bounces a bit.

"Vot do you think zis is? A mattress showroom?"

He loosens his tie. Laughs up at me. I point a finger on his shoulder and push him back. A spring goes boing. This reverse of sex is cooler than it sounds. Something inside instead of inside something. Still, it's not like I was going to let the skunk on top of me. A girl's got standards. No,

I'm the one on top, astride, hands pinning his out and down.

He is gibbering something. I bend down to listen. Now, he says, your heart's desire. Oh, I release him and fly, arms unfolding like wings. This cannot be, this is not my heart's desire. I fold my arms and rest my hands behind my head. I undo the comb. With one swift movement I bring it down with both hands, the tines sinking into his hairless chest.

There is a painting by Jackson Pollock. No, every fucking painting by Jackson Pollock. Jack the Dripper. At last I get it, but I can't take it. The sheer vertigo, the swirling sense of absolute identity. I reel from the bed and gain the landing as if I am being pursued, the stairs spindling down but climbing up forever. I descend to the sound of pealing bells in the rafters, the bats singing to the stars. The stairs are like that Escher print where each person I pass on the stairwell I pass again, flight after flight, each identical: hood drawn up, a face all blank with emptiness. Going up, going up to the pealing bells and the singing bats.

When an eternity passes I reach the lobby, ear-thrilling emptiness funnelling to a door into the street. Cobbled as always, but undulating now to contain the ghastly swell of whatever flows beneath. All up its length, street lamps cast conical spells, each gutter sending steam upwards in nascent tornadoes. I stagger seawards, where that distinctive entropy awaits, of gulls and ozone, a vastness that compels. I must look a mess. But I am not observed. The Department, I recall, releases gas through the gutters in the wee small hours. All abroad fall out of their standing. See them there, stretched on benches, slumbered in doorways, calcified beneath the incessant fallout.

The Chinaman does what the Chinaman does. Maybe he feeds the corpse to the pigs. Maybe he recycles it another way. I make a mental note to avoid the Special Chow Mein. I return to the scene of the crime. The turn-down service has everything pristine. The only clue to their visit provided by a wrapped sweet on the pillow. I pick it up. Written on the gold wrapper are the words: eat me.

I am on my knees and the heaving starts. I hold my hand to my mouth, hoping to keep it all back. Fingers fold around my own. I pull my hand away, straining to look down. The other hand squirms further from my mouth. My jaw is pushed past pain, my head surrenders space to the inner being. I must become a snake, disgorging its prey, all life flows both ways, after all. Now an arm protrudes. I see, through the sharp red pain, a head protrude, its face turned briefly towards mine. The pleasure of recognition. One last push and the creature slides from my mouth and drops in a heap on the ground. I can only stare. The creature coils and twitches in the slime. Slowly it turns. Still I stare.

"How do you think it feels to be stuck inside your head? To live forever in that cavern so vast and empty that you can never be anything but lost. How do you think it feels, to live like a ghost?"

How long have I been resting my head against the mirror? It is densely fogged, but constant staring brings reward. Inscribed by a distillery, mottled with age, obscured by bottles, it offers a panorama of the bar. There are shapes in there, clustered about lights, reflections of reflections that murmur and smile. Someone has drawn a message on the steam. Always you. I close my eyes to think but nothing comes. I open them again to stare into a face hung close that I vaguely recognise. I step back as he sways, waving a finger for some forgotten line. I lean in again and he too leans close. I know what I must tell him as the crowd gathers hush.

"A man walks into a bar ..."

Shane Harrison was born in Dublin. He graduated from the National College of Art and Design in 1982 and has worked in television, advertising and journalism. He lives in Bray, County Wicklow.

www.ingramcontent.com/pod-product-compliance
Lightning Source LLC
Chambersburg PA
CBHW031336060726
47590CB00007B/2496